The UNKINDNESS of STRANGERS

The Hollywood Murder Mysteries

PETER S. FISCHER

THE GROVE POINT PRESS
Pacific Grove, California

Also by Peter S. Fischer
THE BLOOD OF TYRANTS
THE TERROR OF TYRANTS

The Hollywood Murder Mysteries
JEZEBEL IN BLUE SATIN
WE DON'T NEED NO STINKING BADGES
LOVE HAS NOTHING TO DO WITH IT
EVERYBODY WANTS AN OSCAR

ISBN 978-0-9846819-4-5

To Lucille
...who never complains when
I disappear into the office....

CHAPTER ONE

This guy is really getting on my nerves but then, I suppose I asked for it. When Bunny pleaded with me to come with her to this hotsy-totsy soiree, what was I supposed to say? No, thanks. I know it's our last night together. I know I have to fly back to Los Angeles tomorrow morning. And yes, I know it is something you simply must attend, it's part of your job. But on the other hand the Knicks are playing the Celts at the Garden and—I stop. For the briefest of moments I had considered trotting out that last one and instantly thought better of it so here I am in the Grand Ballroom of the Hotel Astor surrounded by the leading lights of New York's literati who are mixing with the nouveau riche and the faux intelligentsia and I am trying to sort out who is who and whether anybody is really having a good time. I know I'm not.

"I just cannot believe that Tom Williams would entrust 'Streetcar' to a tasteless cretin like Jack Warner. Oh, my God, I cringe at the thought."

I have already forgotten this mealy mouthed little weasel's name and now I am looking for a polite way to slip away to more friendly climes. If I can't think of one, I will be rude, but only as a last resort. In addition to being a boor, this guy is also a first class name dropper. Tom Williams, indeed. I, who actually know Tennessee Williams and have been asked by the great man to call him Tom, doubt seriously that this puff pastry in his wine-colored velvet jacket and his robin's egg blue silk ascot has ever been in the same room with him.

"I would hardly call Jack Warner a cretin," I say. "A hard-nosed businessman, yes, but for all his rough edges, he has an instinct for good literature and good film. Don't sell him short."

"Oh, puh-lease," the twerp says. "I have already warned my friends, this will be a watered down version of the play, an innocuous trifle where big sister comes to visit little sister and gets to bantering with beefy brother-in-law. Laughs ensue and the film fades out on a trivial happy ending."

I look past his shoulder and see Bunny hanging on the arm of the mayor, William O'Dwyer. She radiates admiration and awe. The girl knows her stuff. I wonder what she's after. As a sort of assistant-associate editor for Collier's Magazine, she's always on the prowl for a story and O'Dwyer seems to be the target for the night. I check my watch. It should be half time at the Garden. I am also wondering what the score is.

"....and poor Jess Tandy, they treated her like dirt, absolute dirt, dumping her for Vivien Leigh. Vivien Leigh? Oh, my God. English and with all the talent of a baby squid. Could they have done worse?"

"Well, you know, maybe good old Jess Tandy's the lucky one," I say, "I mean, if the movie is going to be as bad as you think it will be."

By now Bunny and the Mayor have been joined by Nelson Rockefeller who has slapped the mayor jocularly on the shoulder. He looks at Bunny, beaming. If he slaps her on her derrierre, I may have to do something about him. Luckily he settles for a handshake.

I look back at the little ferret. His eyes are focused elsewhere. He doesn't look at me but moves off with an abrupt, "Excuse me." His rudeness was much less civil than mine would have been. It's obvious I have put this dilettante in his place and I feel good about it. I grab a flute of champagne from a passing waiter and start to mingle.

The event is being staged to raise funds for some sort of cultural foundation which in turn will disperse money to worthy causes in the arts like ANTA and several acting studios and even individual playwrights and painters and sculptors who have shown promise but haven't put too many bucks in the till as yet. I don't think it ever occurs to these people that grants might be better spent upgrading school facilities or providing work training for the chronically unemployed. But what the hell, maybe the next Picasso or O'Neill is a lot more important and probably a lot more fun to party with.

I wander aimlessly, absorbing the auras of the rich and powerful at play. A string quartet sits atop an elaborate platform that has been erected in the middle of the cavernous hall. They seem fixated on Vivaldi. I have yet to hear anything by Irving Berlin. White haired dowagers festooned with diamonds chat brainlessly with pot bellied captains of industry about trivialities. Juicy tidbits of gossip are passed from clique to clique and back again. Insincere laughter is everywhere. Banalities abound. Am I being too hard on these people? Probably but I know forced gaiety when I see it and this place is crawling with it.

My champagne flute and I wander out onto a terrace that overlooks the city lights below. It's colorful and busy and vibrant and it boasts Broadway and Wall Street so the city can't be all bad but I find it all a little too much. I don't come here because I want to, I come because Bunny is here and Bunny is the woman

I love and right now she is trying to sort out exactly who she is and what she wants out of life. I hope she decides she wants me.

We had been living together for a year back in L.A., she working for The Hollywood Reporter and me working in the press department of Warner Brothers Studios. After a lousy marriage and a worse divorce, I had found her and having found her, I didn't want to let her go. But then she got the offer from Collier's Magazine and after vacillating for months, discovered that she couldn't say no. She needed to find out how good, or how bad, she really was. So now here she is in New York and every other month I fly in to spend five days with her and every other month, she flies to L.A. How's it working out? In all honesty, it isn't. Each month that passes we become more like strangers. While in L.A. with little to do she becomes antsy and bored. In New York I got fed up once I'd done the sights, visited all the museums, and took in a matinee of 'Top Banana'. We talk less now because there's less to talk about.

"Hiya, sailor, looking for a good time?"

I feel her take my arm and I look down and she's smiling up at me with that smile designed to melt a press agent's heart which, believe me, is no easy task.

"What'd you have in mind, babycakes?" I say.

We talk like that a lot. Or at least we used to.

"Had enough of this place?" Bunny asks.

"You're the one on the job, not me," I say.

"Walter knows it's your last night. He told me to take off."

"You sure?" Walter's her boss and, it turns out, a pretty decent guy.

"I was really hoping to talk with Clare Boothe Luce but she looks like a no-show." She tugs at my arm. "Let's get the hell out of here," she says with finality.

We wend our way through the crowd on the way to the elevators. I jostle Robert Alda and wink at Mary Martin, whom I adore, but Bunny's tugging at me relentlessly and I have no time for anything but a goodbye wave. We take the elevator to the lobby and start across just as the lady herself is coming in the main entrance accompanied by her husband Henry. Clare Luce is a little bit of everything including playwright, social activist, journalist and even an Oscar nominee for Fox's "Come to the Stable" two years ago. She's a formidable woman and also very attractive for someone pushing 50.

"Oh,migosh," Bunny says. She looks at me hopefully. "Would you mind, Joe? Just for a minute."

"Go," I smile.

Bunny crosses the lobby at a quick pace and deftly cuts off the great lady before she has a chance to reach the elevator well. Bunny is all smiles and gushes like a Texas geyser. Mrs. Luce graciously abides her and in a moment the two of them are chatting like yentas at a bas mitzvah. Henry is looking around, no doubt trying to spot an open bar. He may have a long wait.

I wander off to admire the opulence of the massive lobby and check out the cute little blonde desk clerk with the Nordic braid down her back. I spot the house dick lounging nonchalantly over by a bank of telephones. His eyes miss nothing, including me. I try to act as if I belong here. I look back toward Bunny and Clare. They're still at it. Henry's checking his watch. It's probably past his bedtime. I can't help remembering a forgettable evening some three years ago when I was divorced and available. An ambitious young actress had lured me into her apartment apparently in the mistaken belief that I was influential enough to help her career. We were in the sack getting ready for some adult recreation when her phone rang. She answered it, then excused herself. This will only take a moment, she says. She then proceeds to spend the next thirty minutes excoriating her agent for getting her lousy interviews for lousy movies and lousier billing when she got the part. Little Joe, who had been standing at attention, lost interest and went to sleep. Consequently, Big Joe got dressed to leave. As I walked out of the room, she didn't even bother to wave goodbye. Outside I got in my car and drove away reminding myself of one of the things my boss Charlie Berger impressed upon me when I first came to work for Warners. He said, do not get romantically involved with actresses or other female impersonators.

I am about to put Bunny into that category when she breaks off the conversation and hurries toward me. She reaches up and gives me a quick kiss on the lips. "You're a darling," she says. "Let's get out of here."

By ten thirty we're back in her tiny apartment in Greenwich Village which overlooks Washington Square. Technically it's not an apartment but a studio which means that there is no bedroom and the sofa I am sitting on turns magically into a double bed. The magic has not yet occurred so I am relaxing at one end swilling a Rheingold beer (no Coors east of the Rockies) and Bunny is at the other end, sipping on some cold leftover coffee from breakfast. She is furiously taking notes on a yellow lined legal pad.

"Fanny Brice is dead," she says.

Bunny is a master of the non-sequitor but this one is a doozy.

"Is she?" I say.

"Clare says she just heard the news. Fanny was fifty-nine."

"Ah," I say.

"I'm almost thirty," Bunny points out. Another non-sequitor.

"You are," I say.

"Fanny was nineteen when she went to work for Flo Zeigfeld."

"Wow," I say.

"Nineteen, Joe," she whines. "And I'm almost thirty."

"I think we covered that."

"Nineteen and starring in the Follies and I'm thirty and no place."

"Almost thirty," I remind her, "and you are someplace. You are writing for a prestigious national magazine."

She glares at me. "I hustle coffee for men who write for a prestigious national magazine."

"You exaggerate."

"Yes, I do," she says adamantly.

"I think you are writing right now," I say.

"Yes, I am," she snaps.

"Want to tell me about it or do I have to wait and buy a copy of the magazine?"

She glares at me. "Don't minimize me, Joe," she says.

"I'm not. Tell me what you have."

She hesitates, then says, "Mrs. Luce is working behind the scenes to get the Republican nomination for Eisenhower."

"She told you that?" I say.

"No, she denied it," Bunny says, "but it's the way she denied it. I got the same kind of denial from Tom Dewey."

"I didn't know Ike was a Republican," I say.

"Maybe he's not. I hear Truman met with him and pressured him to compete for the Democratic nomination."

"Sounds odd," I say.

"Sure, until you figure Harry is trying to preempt MacArthur from getting nominated any time, any place, any ticket. They say Harry's still galled over the Korea business."

"Well, whatever ticket Ike chooses to run on, he wins hands down. He's one politician I could genuinely like. As for the others, I wouldn't trade you a spittoon of spit for the whole damned lot of them."

Bunny looks over at me. "Some of them are decent, hardworking patriots."

"Yeah? Name two."

She shrugs. "They grow on you."

"Barnacles grow on ship's hulls. So what?"

"You really are a cynic," she says.

"Realist," I say. "You and Walt and the others live in a world that could explode within minutes, where one madman could erase centuries of a cultured civilization and our self-serving politicians pretend that nothing is wrong. I live in a world of make-believe. Given a choice, most people would rather live in my world."

"People must be made to understand the truth," she says fervently.

I look over at her sharply. "They know the truth, Bunny, and they don't need 'Life' or 'Look' or 'Colliers' to tell them what that truth is. They know the bomb is hanging over us like Damocles' sword. They know that the best and the brightest of our youngest generation are being slaughtered by the thousands in a godforsaken mountainous piece of rock they'd never even heard of two years ago. And they also know that they haven't the faintest idea why we are doing all this."

"The Communist aggressors must be----"

"Yeah, I've heard all that and it's hooey. If you believe that then we'll be fighting little wars all over the world for the next fifty years and still be wondering why."

She looks at me quietly for a few moments. "How did we get on this subject?" she asks.

"With great difficulty," I say. "Let's get off of it."

She puts down her pad and squiggles her way across the sofa until she is in my arms. I hold her tight and kiss her and she responds. It's almost as heartfelt as it used to be. Very soon we are unclothed and satisfying one another and it is good. It is very good but it isn't the same as what we once had and we both know it.

Early the next morning she drives me to LaGuardia to catch the 8:15 TWA to Los Angeles. Traffic is light. The suburbanites who are silly enough to drive to work are headed the other way. We are mostly quiet. What conversation there is is sporadic and shallow. She has her thoughts. I have mine. There are a thousand things I want to say, a thousand questions I want to ask but now is not the time. She's changed, no question about that, but how? Is she smarter, more seasoned, more aware or herself and the world around her. I have no right to object to that. I was forged in the crucible of war. Bunny has never known real doubt or discomfort or uncertainty. Now she is being challenged in the most competitive environment in the world. And if she is growing, what am I doing? Am I turning dull and predictable in a comfortable non-threatening job. Did my vistas stop expanding six years ago and if so, what does that say about our future together?

She parks the car and we go into the terminal. I buy my ticket and check my bag and we make our way to Gate 21. We have a few minutes to spare so I buy a paperback copy of 'The Wall' by John Hersey. I know I'll probably fall asleep before we hit Ohio but I buy it anyway. Finally they call my flight. I think we're both relieved. I put my arms around her and hold her close. As we separate I look into her eyes. I don't know why I say it. I hadn't meant to. It just came out.

"What's going to happen to us, babe?" I say.

She looks at me, eyes reflecting the turmoil within. I think I see tears starting to well up.

"I don't know," she says quietly and then she turns and hurries away and, sadly, I watch her go.

CHAPTER TWO

've picked a window seat so I can watch the country go by below. The DC-4 isn't crowded. Half full. Maybe 45 or 50 passengers. The stewardess is young, attractive and attentive. At this hour I have no need of a drink but I do get a nice glass of orange juice and a sunny smile. Below me the Empire State Building is reaching up to touch our wingtips but it never gets close. I think I see Broadway but I'm not sure. Lady Liberty still looks good and still gives me a patriotic shiver as she guards the nation's doorway, her torch held high. We fly over the Hudson, the George Washington Bridge visible to the north and then it is behind me and I am looking at the suburbs and farmlands of northern Jersey. I expect to be back in ten or eleven weeks. Part of me is not sure about that, the way things were left between Bunny and me. I feel a knot in my stomach. I don't want to think about it nor do I want to think about what's waiting for me back at the studio but I have no choice.

Ever since Jack Warner got involved with "A Streetcar Named Desire", I've been living in a bad dream. Of late it's become a nightmare. It starts with Tennessee Williams' play. From coast to coast come the screams of disbelief from critics and pundits of every description. How in God's name will you be able to film something so lascivious, so grimy, so disgusting, so—The adjectives roll out in newsprint and through the ether via radio and television. This play of debauchery cannot be filmed. Jack Warner has lost his mind. It is my job, and the job of my boss, Charlie Berger, to refute this criticism but when you are dealing with hardline come-to-Jesus fundamentalists it's almost impossible.

Technically, I suppose, 'Streetcar' is not a full blown Warner Brothers product. A guy named Charles Feldman has the rights and has made some sort of deal with the studio. I'm not a business affairs guy so I don't know the details and frankly I don't care. What I do know is that Jack Warner has a lot of input into this project and he doesn't mind throwing his weight around. Warner is adamant as well as stubborn and he has made up his mind. America will see this play on film and the critics and the censors and the Catholic Church be damned.

As of five days ago when I left LA. there had been 60 script changes, with more to come, most of which are intended to eviscerate the core of Williams' work. The crucial piece in this confrontation of wills is the censorship board. Without a seal of approval, the film cannot be released. Period. Fortunately, we have a couple of things on our side. Setting aside the nature of it's content, the play is an acknowledged work of art. The censors would prefer not to be known as tasteless, hidebound barbarians without a lick of artistic judgement. Secondly, films from Italy and Sweden have been breaking all sorts of adult-themed barriers for the past five or six years and happily, the world hasn't gone to hell with itself. We may not have an Ingmar Bergman or a Federico Fellini at the helm but we do have Elia Kazan and that's pretty darned good.

A lot of Williams' vision is gone. Blanche's young husband, a homosexual, is now described as weak. In addition Blanche's rapacious love of sex for its own sake is now clouded in vagueness and euphemisms. And finally the censors had categorically forbidden any hint of rape in the final scene between Stanley and Blanche. On this last point Warner and Kazan dug in their heels. The scene will be filmed or they will walk away, humiliate the censors in the press and possibly even institute legal action. This latter threat terrifies the censors because they realize should Warners prevail, the floodgates will open and anything will go. The last I heard the rape scene was approved but in an artistic and non-specific staging.

As far as I know the only thing left open for discussion is how the final scene will be shot and both sides are working toward a compromise.

"Joe?"

I hear my name and look up. Ted Loesch is leaning toward me, smiling.

"I thought it was you. I was sitting in the back trying to grab some shuteye."

Ted is my counterpart at MGM and a genuinely nice guy. We've shared a few brews together at industry functions and even ducked out in tandem to find a watering hole less clouded with movieland politics.

"Pull up a seat," I say.

"Thanks. It's been hours since I've talked with an actual human being. You'll do." He waves to the cute stew who hurries to our side. Ted orders a Jack Daniels neat and since he hates to drink alone, I break down and ask for a beer. It's Schlitz in a can and it'll do.

"So, in New York for business?" I ask.

"Just one day, reporting to the brass. Been in D.C. since Thursday," he says.

"What's in Washington?" I ask.

"HUAC," he says bitterly. He downs half the glass.

"Bad news?"

"Bad enough," he replies.

HUAC is the House Un-American Actiivities Committee and they've been chasing bogeymen in Hollywood ever since 1947. In the Senate Joe McCarthy is chasing Commies in politics and the military. The House has a character named John Stephens Wood, a Democrat from Georgia, who is certain that suspect writers and performers in the movies are hellbent on destroying the fabric of America. 1951 marks a new push in that direction and there is palpable fear in many quarters of what Congressman John Stephens Wood may uncover. As for me, I don't know any Commies. At least I don't think I do. Occasionally I check to see if some new acquaintance is wearing an armband featuring a red star but so far, no sign of one. The one thing I do know, however, is that this bunch of narcissistic Congressional clowns have ruined a lot of lives, many of them innocent bystanders to this government sponsored madness. For the most part I try not to think about it. Call me selfish but I can't save the world. Hell, right now, I can't even save myself.

"How bad is bad," I ask, "or is that confidential?"

He drains his glass and signals to the stew for another.

"Larry Parks," he says. "They had him on the hot seat a few weeks back. Really worked him over. I have no idea if he's a pinko or not. I doubt it but you know how it was in the thirties."

I shake my head in ignorance. "My high school years."

"Country going to hell. Government's useless. Everybody's looking for answers. The Commies start recruiting. A lot of guys showed up at meetings out of curiosity or to meet girls. Most never went back. That's where I'd put Larry but these assholes in Congress never see it that way. Poor bastard. I feel for him."

"Where's the studio come in?" I ask.

"We just finished a picture with Larry and Elizabeth Taylor. Cute little comedy, nothing more. The studio's scared shitless. They may be looking at really bad press and no business. They sent me to talk to Wood and his gang to give Larry a clean slate. They weren't interested. Larry's a big catch for them. They're keeping him."

I shake my head. "Lousy," I say.

"Yeah and who knows who else they have on their radar? Larry's wife Betty Garrett for sure. The way things are you're scared stiff to make a decision. This actor, that screenwriter, all of a sudden you're in bed with so-called Commies and you never saw it coming." Half his second glass goes down the gullet. "You guys got lucky with Kazan," he continues.

I look at him, puzzled.

"Kazan? What about him?"

"He's on their list."

"I'd heard that but he told us there was nothing to worry about."

"Of course not," Ted says. "He's going to cooperate."

"What do you mean? Name names?"

"Sure. What do you think I mean?" Ted says. "Hey, maybe I'm wrong but it's what I hear and I'm not the only one."

I try to picture Kazan sitting at a table in front of the bank of Congressmen, ratting out people he has known for at least a decade. It doesn't come easy.

"I think you're wrong," I say.

"Maybe I am. I hope so. The business needs people like Gadge." Those who know him and even some who don't call him 'Gadge'. They have for years. Why, I have no idea.

Ted tosses back the rest of his drink and excuses himself. He's going to try to stretch out on the back row and grab some sleep. I wish him luck. I could use some myself but I'm too hopped up to doze off. Too many things are buzzing around in my brain and I can't get rid of them.

The Commie scare isn't the only thing wrong in Hollywood these days though it's probably the second most important. Number one by far is the loss of audience. Five years ago, right after the war, sixty million people a year went to the movies. That was down from the boom years of the Thirties but still it was very good and everybody was making money. But for the past five years, attendance has been on a downward slide. The onslaught of television is part of it. Television is free in the comfort of your home and you don't have to hire a babysitter. Sure, it's in black and white and the screen is small and the actors are even smaller but the folks just don't seem to care. And then there's the rush to the suburbs, away from the huge downtown theaters, replaced by smaller outlets in shopping malls and with far fewer seats. That's a big part of it.

And finally there's the product, basically no worse than it has always been but in many ways, no better either. But the audience has changed. G.I.'s back from the war who were naive high schoolers now know better and the women who marched into the factories and turned out the planes and ships and tanks, they're not the same either. The town I love is under siege from many different directions and the men who run the studios are going to have to react and change or the industry could be doomed.

Not a pretty thought, I think, as my eyes close and I drift off to sleep.

CHAPTER THREE

ednesday morning. I awaken very early and grab a quick bite at the local diner before heading for the studio. I remind myself to stop at the grocery store on the way home and pick up provisions. When I flew to New York I left the cupboard bare.

I half expected to find my desk littered with unread mail and piles of memos but Glenda Mae, the former Mississippi beauty queen who now toils as my gal Friday, has dealt with just about everything on her own initiative. Five letters and three memos are all that are left. These I can handle. It's not yet eight-thirty so I decide to wander over to Sound Stage 12 where a slice of New Orleans is being recreated.

There was a time when it looked as if we'd be flying in to New Orleans to shoot a lot of exterior scenes. It seemed logical. Stage plays are cramped. Films are wide open, more often than not featuring photogenic vistas to establish time and place. Kazan wrestled with the idea for many weeks and finally decided against it. He felt obligated to honor the claustrophobic nature of Williams play so he opted to build the exterior of the apartment building on one of the sound stages assigned to the picture. The few concessions to reality would be some minimal footage from New

Orleans like the opening shot at the railway station, the reveal of the streetcar with its destination, "Desire", prominently featured , and a short early scene in a bowling alley. Just about everything else would be created on a sound stage at the studio.

I open the door to the stage and am assaulted by the sounds of hammers hammering and saws sawing. I'm hoping to find Kazan so I can subtly, I hope, query him about any possible testimony before the House committee. Kazan is at the helm of a very controversial, very expensive motion picture. Were he to publicly run afoul of the House committee or lose the favor of the movie going public, it could cost the studio millions in lost revenue. It's my job to make sure that doesn't happen.

Inside the sound stage, the elaborate courtyard set seems to be coming along nicely. I don't see Kazan but I do spot Richard Day, the art director, who's into heavy conversation with the construction foreman. He sees me and waves. I wander over just as the foreman is leaving.

"So, what do you think?" Day asks with a smile as he jabs a thumb toward the construction.

"Top notch as usual," I reply.

"Yes, the boys are getting it right like they always do. We'll be ready." He sees me peering around. "Anything I can do for you, Joe?"

"I was hoping to run into Kazan," I say.

"Just left. Man's a nervous wreck. The third time in two days he's checked on the walls."

I look at him blankly. "The walls?"

"The walls in the apartment. You didn't hear? He wants them put on rollers so he can tighten them up in the later scenes."

"Call me a dunce, Richard, but you've lost me."

"We're going to cheat a little, Joe. The crazier Blanche gets, the more the walls of the apartment will seem to close in on her. Well, that's what Gadge wants, for the walls to literally close in on her toward the end of the picture and especially in the rape scene."

I nod appreciatively. "Clever. Must be why we pay him the big bucks."

"Guess so," Day says. "By the way, sorry about what happened to your friend."

I frown in ignorance. "What happened to what friend?"

"The columnist from the Times. Ogilvy. Someone beat the bejesus out of him late Friday evening."

"You're kidding," I say, disbelieving. Phineas Ogilvy is the last person I'd ever expect to be in a brawl.

"No, it was in the paper Saturday morning."

"Well, how is he?"

"Okay as far as I know. I think they kept him overnight in the hospital and let him go in the morning." He looks past me. "'Scuse me, Joe. I'm needed. If I see Gadge I'll tell him you were looking for him."

He leaves while I try to assimilate the improbable. Perplexed I start back to my office. As I'm going, he's coming. I've never met Karl Malden but I'd know him anywhere. He's a bear of a man with a broad friendly smile and a nose as big as the state of Montana.

"Mr. Malden," I say as we draw near to one another. He smiles. I introduce myself and we shake hands. When he learns I'll be working press and publicity, he promises total cooperation.

"I don't suppose you've seen Mr. Kazan," I say.

"Someone told me I'd find him on Stage 12. That's where I'm headed," Malden says.

"I just came from there. He left about thirty minutes ago. No telling where he went."

"Too bad. I haven't seen Gadge in almost a year. Thought we'd catch up on things."

"I understand you two were close before the war, back in New York," I say.

"That we were. Group Theater. A lot of us got our starts there. Great friends, great fun and great training. A little sparse in the compensation area. We used to say we were starving to death but having fun doing it." His face becomes more serious. "Terrible what they're doing in Washington. They make it seem like everyone back then was a subversive. It wasn't like that at all."

"You ever attend one of those meetings?" I ask.

"No, I didn't have time for that stuff. I'd just gotten married. Unless I was working, I stayed home with Mona."

"How about Kazan?" I ask.

Malden's smile fades. "Why do you want to know?"

"Because I heard he was going to be called up in front of the committee."

Malden nods. "Yes, I'd heard that, too."

"I've also heard he was going to cooperate."

Malden hesitates. "I wouldn't know anything about that. Look, Mr. Bernardi---"

"Joe. Please."

"Joe. Gadge is no Communist. Maybe he went to a few meetings but if so, it never stuck. I know the man. We've been close since the first day we met. If he's cooperating, I'm sure he has his reasons."

"That's why I need to talk to him. My job is to run interference and put a good face on things but I can't deal with the media if I'm flying blind."

"Of course you can't," Malden says. "If I see him, I'll tell him you're looking for him. Meantime I'm going to sightsee. My first time on this lot. Got a lot of history going for it."

"That it does," I say and I watch him go. It's only our first encounter but I already like the guy a lot.

Back at the office I find Glenda Mae sorting the mail. She throws me a welcome back smile. I throw it right back at her and ask her to get me Phineas at the L.A Times where he reigns as the city's preeminent entertainment columnist.

"Ogilvy," he growls, picking up the phone.

Uh-oh. Bad mood. Guess I shouldn't be surprised.

"What the hell happened?" I ask.

He knows my voice. "Joseph, dear friend. Many thanks for calling so quickly to check on my condition."

"I was in New York the past few days, you pompous narcissist. So, what happened?"

A moment's silence. Then he asks, "Do you have an luncheon engagement?"

"No."

"The Formosa. Twelve-thirty. I'm buying. Don't be late."

He hangs up. My curiosity has been heightened a dozen notches. Not only a face to face but he's buying. This promises to be very interesting.

I buzz Glenda Mae and ask her to get me my boss, Charlie Berger. She tells me that Charlie won't be in until after lunch. He has an eleven o'clock appointment at the St. Sebastian private school in West L.A., one of the city's newest top tier coed private schools. Right away I get it. He's looking for a first class place to stash his twin six year olds, Daphne and Danielle. Normally this chore would have fallen to his wife, Alicia, who is no longer on the scene. A 27 year old trophy wife when he married her nine years ago, Alicia has decided that motherhood is not her forte and has moved into a suite at the Roosevelt which Charlie is paying for. Divorce is imminent. Meanwhile Charlie has two little girls to look after and hasn't a clue. He's hired a housekeeper and a governess but it's not enough. Each morning he comes to work greyer and gaunter than he was the day before. Charlie was supposed to retire at the end of last year but under the circumstances decided to stay on. As he told me several months ago, it was either keep working or stay home and blow a hole in his head.

I tell Glenda Mae to leave word I called and I get to the business of clearing paperwork off my desk.

The Formosa Cafe is one of the old quirky movie biz landmarks. It's been around for at least twenty years and so has its owner Lem Quon who knows just about everyone who is anyone and is quick with a smile of greeting. The area nearest the entrance is large and decorated with dozens of photos of stars, new and old. Last week the Formosa made the papers when the cops walked in and arrested gangster Mickey Cohen in the middle of lunch. This is what you call authentic local color.

The rear of the cafe is a remodeled railroad dining car which is where Lem seats me. I'm the first to arrive and I order a beer. When Phineas arrives I recognize him despite the fact that some of his face has been rearranged. A shiner is just clearing up, he has a bad bruise on his jaw line and a flesh colored bandage covers some sort of wound on his forehead. It is obvious Phineas is mortified. Every day of the year he is elegantly dressed, his longish hair coiffed immaculately, his face closely shaven and he smells of expensive cologne. Those who do not know him assume immediately that this outgoing flamboyant man is homosexual but they are wrong and Phineas has three ex-wives and four children to prove it. My theory is that each of his wives resented being the less beautiful half of the marriage but that is only a theory. I have heard faint rumors that Phineas is on the prowl for wife number four but if so, his current visage isn't going to help much.

As Lem seats him, Phineas orders a double Gibson. For Phineas this is tantamount to binge drinking. Normally he drinks white wine in small quantities. This is not a happy man.

"Feel free to stare at my wounds to your heart's content, Joseph, and then stop. It's enough that I know I look freakish. You needn't remind me of it all through lunch."

"Never entered my mind but seeing you like this is a bit incongruous. What happened?"

He raises a hand. "First my drink, then we order and then I divulge all."

His Gibson comes. He orders a Cobb salad. I settle for a patty melt and fries. Then he gets to it.

"It was nearly midnight. I had returned to my apartment house, parked my car and was walking toward the entrance when two men stepped in front of me. Before I could react this huge rhinoceros of a man with a grotesque birthmark the size of Delaware under his eye hit me in the stomach. Joe, I tell you, I have never known such pain. I doubled over and felt as if I was about to regurgitate when he hit me hard across the face. By that time, the other man had grabbed my arms and was holding them tight. I was helpless as the man's fists kept pounding at me. Finally he stopped. The man holding me let me fall to the ground. One last kick to my ribs and then they walked away."

"Did they say anything?"

"Not a word. It wasn't a holdup, old top. I had several hundred dollars in my pocket and a thousand dollar Piaget on my wrist."

"Then what was it?" I ask.

"Retaliation. Intimidation."

"You know who these men were?"

"No, but I know who sent them."

"Who?"

"Have you heard of Bryce Tremayne?"

"Sounds vaguely familiar. Some sort of reporter."

"Columnist. Works for the San Antonio Express News. Hearst syndicates him throughout the country." He takes a deep sip of his drink, then extracts the onions and pops them into his mouth. He winces. I think the bruise on his jaw hurts more than he lets on.

"I was at a press party at Paramount. DeMille had invited a few of us to screen some scenes from the circus picture he's been working on. You know DeMille's politics. Tremayne is cut from the same bolt of cloth only more so. Well, really, what can you expect from a Hearst acolyte? Anyway, I suppose I'd had one too many chardonnays so when Tremayne and I started discussing the Hollywood witch hunt, I gently chided him for writing a favorable piece about HUAC's chairman John Stephens Wood."

"Gentle? Chiding?" I say in disbelief. No criticism from Phineas Ogilvy has ever been gentle.

Phineas hesitates, taking another belt of his drink. "Perhaps gentle is a tad inaccurate. Now that I recall I think I made some reference that reflected badly on his mother." I nod knowingly. "I also may have uttered a negative reference to his cognitive powers." I nod again. "And oh, yes, I think I let slip that I thought he had the moral scruples of Adolph Eichmann."

I smile. "Was this all in one long drawn out sentence or did you let him get a word in edgewise?"

"Don't remember, but I'll tell you this, old top, afterwards I felt like Jesus must have felt after he tossed the money lenders out of the temple."

"And how do you feel now, Phineas?"

At this moment Lem appears with our luncheons. Phineas

raises his hands. "Enough," he says. "As agreed, no discussion of this topic during lunch."

I think back and try to remember when the "as agreed" part was agreed upon. It hadn't been but I don't care. I attack my patty melt with enthusiasm. Phineas picks at his salad cautiously and I can see that every bite is an ordeal. For a man with a Mensa-level I.Q., Phineas can sometimes do very dumb things.

By the time I get back to the office, Charlie is looking for me. Frantically, Glenda Mae says. That I doubt. Charlie gets agitated but never frantic. I hurry down to the opposite end of the long corridor were Charlie holds sway and pop into his private sanctum, smiling.

"How much?" I ask.

"How much what?" he glares.

"How much per kid?"

The glare intensifies. "Do you actually know everything that takes place within the walls of this studio or just those that concern my personal life?"

"Mostly the latter," I say.

He lights up an Old Gold from a half-crushed package he retrieves from his shirt pocket and takes a long drag.

"Nineteen hundred dollars," he says.

"For two?"

"Each," he growls. He takes another long drag on the cigarette. "I'm going to kill that woman," he says. "She's got me smoking again after twenty- two years. Maybe I'll drop dead of lung cancer just to spite her."

"It'll take more than cigarettes to kill you, Charlie. You're much too stubborn," I say.

He ignores me.

'How was New York?" he asks.

"Great," I say.

"I doubt it," he responds. "Coast to coast romances never work out, Joe. Take my advice. Get on with your life. Much as I like Bunny, don't let some dame drag you around by your pecker. It always ends badly. I should know. You're looking at People's Exhibit One."

Uh-oh. Charlie's slipping into his I-feel-sorry-for-myself mode. In a minute he'll be breaking out the scotch and I'll have to join him and we'll both be blotto by lunchtime.

"Glenda Mae said you had something urgent for me," I say, prodding him to return to reality.

"Yeah," he says, fumbling around on his desk, sifting through the papers strewn there. "Gotta guy wants to interview Kazan. Kazan wants no part of him. I'm electing you to run interference."

He finds a sheet of paper and squints at it. "Yeah, this is him. A real son of a bitch, this guy. I'd say blow him off but he represents over a hundred and fifty papers so we have to play nice. Give him anything he wants except Kazan. If he gets nasty, live with it. If he gets really nasty, then fuck him."

He hands me the sheet of paper.

I see Charlie has written down Biltmore Hotel and a phone number and the guy's name.

Captain America.

"What the hell is this, Charlie?"

"It's a secret password straight out of a Nick Carter decoder ring. When you call the Biltmore you give them this name. This bastard is so egotistical he thinks if he registers under his own name everyone in L.A. will be calling him."

"And when I get this Captain America on the phone who will I actually be talking to?"

"Sorry. Didn't I tell you? His name's Tremayne. Bryce Tremayne."

CHAPTER FOUR

When the operator at the Biltmore says, "Biltmore Hotel, how may I help you?", it's all I can do to keep a straight face.

"Captain America, please," I say.

Deadpan, she responds. "Is that a staff member or a guest, sir?"

"A guest," I say.

"One moment, please." There is silence , then a ring followed by a second ring. A man answers.

"Yes?"

"Captain America, please."

"Who's calling?"

I can't resist. "Lamont Cranston," I say.

"Just a moment," the man says without missing a beat. I can't believe it. Apparently this lunkhead has never listened to even one episode of 'The Shadow'. After a lengthy pause another man comes on the line.

"Hello."

"Is this Captain America?" I ask.

"No, this is Captain Marvel. Who are you? Clark Kent?"

"Not at the moment," I say with a chuckle.

"Didn't think so." He's also chuckling. His voice is deep and twangy and as Texas as twin tumbleweeds hopping along the prairie. "This is Bryce. Who the hell are you?"

I tell him my name and where I'm from.

"Nice talking to you, Mr. Bernardi. You got Kazan standing there next to you?"

"No. Mr. Kazan is temporarily unavailable."

"How about you call back when he IS available."

I can sense him starting to hang up so I talk fast.

"He won't be, Mr. Tremayne, not until I've talked to you first."

"I don't work that way," he says.

"I do," I say.

There's a long pause while Tremayne considers his options.

"You a drinkin' man, Mr. Bernardi?" he asks.

"I've been known to make a few beers disappear now and then."

"Good. My suite at the Biltmore. Six-double O- One. Five o'clock. Bring Kazan if you can, otherwise you'll do." He hangs up.

By four-thirty I'm on the road, heading over the ridge that divides Los Angeles from the San Fernando Valley. I turn toward downtown and in a matter of minutes I pull up to the imposing edifice known as The Biltmore Hotel. Built nearly thirty years ago, its Spanish Italian Renaissance architecture is awe inspiring. Presidents and Kings have stayed here. Not one has publicly complained about anything. I leave my car with the valet, duck inside, and walk briskly across the thickly carpeted lobby to the elevator well. At five o'clock precisely I push the button next to the double doors that guard suite 6001 and a moment later they open.

My greeter is a big man, at least six-two and maybe two forty. I'm pretty sure that very little of that two forty is body fat. His complexion is sallow and he could use a good dentist. He also has a prominent delta-shaped purple birthmark on his left cheek right below his eye. Although I am not a trained detective

I believe I have identified the behemoth that rearranged Phineas Ogilvy's facial features.

He doesn't smile but gestures for me to open my suit jacket wide. Satisfied that I am not packing, he leads me into the suite which is, like the rest of the hotel, predictably lavish. We walk by a second man who hasn't taken his eyes off me since we walked in. He's skinny with a long narrow face and a needle nose and ears that pop out at right angles. I smile in greeting. He doesn't bother to smile back.

I spot a pudgy gentleman by the window, drink in hand, looking out at the traffic below. He has curly blonde hair and his face seems reddish. When I look close there are little blood vessels that have come to the surface courtesy of an alcohol diet. This marshmallow of a man cannot possibly be Bryce Tremayne. Neither can the woman standing behind the bar refilling her glass. Within a moment or two the Man himself emerges from the bedroom, slim with dark wavy hair and deep set hawklike eyes that take in everything and concede nothing. He smiles as he walks toward me, hand outstretched. The smile seems genuine but the eyes refute it. They are cold and searching for weakness.

"Welcome, Mr. Bernardi," he says, grasping my hand. "Bryce Tremayne." His grip is strong and he pumps once for emphasis before letting go. Then his arm is around my shoulder as he leads me to the sofa where he bids me sit.

"I believe you said beer on the phone," he says.

"I did," I say.

He signals to the big doorman. "Willie, bring Mr. Bernardi a cold one. Glass?" he asks me.

"Bottle's fine," I say.

"Just the bottle, Willie," Tremayne says as he plops himself down into an easy chair opposite me. There's a cedar humidor on the table and he shoves it toward me. "Have a cigar. Havanas. The best. I don't smoke but I carry 'em around for friends and guests."

I shake my head. "I don't smoke either," I say.

He leans back in the chair and gives me the once-over.

"So, it's not every day I get a chance to share drinks with an honest to God author," he says.

I look at him incredulously. "You've read my book?"

"Not yet. My secretary picked it up this afternoon at a bookshop. I'll dig into it tonight."

"I'm flattered," I say.

He smiles. "I like to know who I'm doin' business with. Sorry you didn't sell more copies. I hear you got some good reviews."

I shrug. "Reviews don't pay the mortgage."

I squirm a little. My book's a sore subject. Barry Loeb, my agent, found a decent second tier publisher who was willing to take a chance on the material. The initial run was five thousand copies. At last count we'd sold less than a thousand. Faced with the public's tepid reaction, Warner's declined to take an option, even though the Casper (Wyoming) Star Tribune called it the best first time novel since 'The Naked and the Dead'. And I thought the movie business was tough.

Willie brings the drinks. Beer for me. Something brown with ice cubes for Tremayne. He raises his glass, I raise my bottle and we drink.

"So, Joe," he says, "why is it that Mr. Kazan doesn't care to talk to me?"

"First hand, I don't know. I haven't talked to him. Maybe it's the difference in your politics."

He roars with laughter. "Politics? Hell, I don't give a damn about politics. I'm a patriot, Joe. That's my politics. Whoever's standin' up for this country, he's got my vote. Yes, sir. Labels don't mean a damned thing to me. Country first and last."

He looks past me toward the bar and the broad grin turns to a scowl.

"Elvira, what the hell are you doing over there?" he barks.

I turn to look. The woman at the bar tries a smile. "Just having a drink, Bryce honey," she says. For the first time I notice that her right eye is darker than the other. She's tried unsuccessfully to hide it with makeup.

"Hell," he says, "that's number four or five. Too damned many. Put it down and go in the bedroom."

"But, darling----"

"Damn it, woman, you got a hearing problem? Get rid of the damned drink and go into the bedroom. Now." When she hesitates, Tremayne looks at the big man. "Willie!" He jerks his head toward the woman.

"No, it's all right. I'm going," she says pushing her glass aside and then moving quickly toward the bedroom door. She goes in and closes the door behind her.

"Got me a good woman there," Tremayne says, "when she's sober. Ain't as often as it used to be. Guess she's got the failing. Irish, you know. On her mother's side. Not a whole lot you can do about it."

I smile politely. "Maybe we should get to the reason you asked me here, Mr. Tremayne."

"Sure, son. Be happy to. In a couple of weeks, maybe a month, they'll be haulin' Mr. Elia Kazan's ass in front of the committee. Before they do I want to make sure that America knows exactly who that Commie son of a bitch is and what he stands for."

"I see," I say. "And given your position, do you really think

Mr.Kazan is going to sit still for a grilling for a column that you've already written?"

"I'm not close minded, Joe. If he has something worthwhile to say I'll print it. "

"Yes, I'm sure you will," I say with more than a trace of sarcasm.

"Look, son, I don't have to extend him any kind of courtesy. My research is accurate. I've got names, dates and places and I will expose him for the traitorous Communist that he is."

"You're wrong. He's no Communist."

"I'm sure that's what he told you," Tremayne scoffs.

"No, except for a couple of conference meetings, I've never actually talked to the man but I have talked to people who know him and who knew him in the years before the war."

"Yes, yes, I read you, son. He's got friends. Good old boys who'll swear he only went to those meetings out of curiosity. Didn't know what they were all about. Walked out right away soon as he saw they were a bunch of Reds and never went back. And then my personal favorite, he only went to meet girls."

"Doubtful," I say. "He was married at the time."

Tremayne's eyes narrow and they lose their humor.

"Now you listen to me, son. Don't you get all hissy with me. I'm doin' God's work here. These traitorous Commie lovers have the access to poison the minds of millions of people, kids especially, who think they are just seeing a movie. Turn your back and these bastards'll slip in an America-hatin' message every chance they get. Well, they ain't gettin' that chance, not as long as I got breath enough left to stop 'em. Now don't you sell me short, boy. I ain't kiddin' here, not by a jugful. I've got me the power to break you and Kazan and all those other smug pinkos over at your studio. You fool with me and I'll wake snakes till Hell won't have it, you get me?"

I shake my head. "I doubt you'll have much luck intimidating Mr. Warner."

He laughs. "You think not? I wasn't born in the woods to be scared by an owl, son. You know how many papers carry my column? You know how many readers I've got?"

"Oh. Some of your followers can read. Excellent!"

"Be snide if you like, Mr. Bernardi, but I asked you here in a spirit of cooperation----"

"Bullshit! I'm here because you thought maybe you could bully me into getting Kazan to sit still for a phony interview in which you could humiliate and insult him. Well, that isn't going to happen."

He is about to respond when I see that his attention has been drawn to something behind me. I turn to see a slender young woman standing by the open door to a second bedroom which I surmise may have been turned into some sort of office. In her hand are several sheets of paper and she is signalling to him. At her side is a slim young man with thinning red hair and wearing very thick rimless eye glasses. It's my guess he couldn't locate the watch on his wrist without them.

"Scuse me," Tremayne says, rising and going to the bedroom door. The three of them confer for a few moments while Tremayne scans several pages of documents, then he walks over to the large dining table and starts to sign the papers. The red-headed guy points out where his signatures should go. Meanwhile, the woman looks at me and when I meet her gaze, she doesn't look away. She seems plain though I don't think she has to be. Her makeup is minimal and her hairdo is dowdy and the dress she is wearing is serviceable and not much more. I smile. She smiles back and then turns her attention back to Tremayne who hands her the signed papers. She goes back into the bedroom as Tremayne and the redhead chat briefly, their backs to us. Whatever they are discussing it's intense. The redhead then nods and heads toward the door. I look over at the pudgy guy by the window and realize he has been watching the redhead intently. He, too, moves to the doorway to intercept the redhead. He says something I can't hear. The redhead shakes his head. Pudgy grabs his arm. The redhead yanks it away and goes out. By now Tremayne has caught this exchange and he's annoyed.

"God damn it, Hubbell, we're doing business here. It'll keep," Tremayne says.

Pudgy starts to say something then thinks better of it and walks over to the bar to fix himself another drink. Tremayne starts back to his chair and as he does, he looks over at his hulking bodyguard and twirls his finger. "Willie!" he calls out. Willie nods and heads for the bar to fetch fresh drinks. One thing these Texans know how to do is put away their booze.

"Not much to look at," Tremayne says , "but she's sharp."

"Excuse me," I say.

"My Jenny. I saw you looking her over, son. I couldn't tie my shoes without her so you just leave her be, hear?" He smiles as he says it. Just then Willie hands him a fresh drink and me a fresh uncapped bottle of beer. I haven't finished the first one so I put it down on the coffee table.

"Now, we were saying---" Tremayne says as if it's a question.

"You know damned well what we were saying," I tell him.

He nods. "Yes. Mr. Kazan's refusal to meet with me. Well, no matter. I'll just have to let my folks out there know I tried to get Mr. Elia Kazan's side of the story but he was afraid to expose himself to my scrutiny. You see, Joe, if old Elia and I talk, I win. If we don't, I also win."

I stare at the man. He may be smiling but he reminds me of a cobra. Who was it said that power corrupts and absolute power corrupts absolutely? The man claims to be a journalist but he is not. He claims to speak for the people but he doesn't. He is a vicious bully with a typewriter and a forum. I'm reminded of Benito Mussolini who started his career as a newspaper reporter and ended up a vile twisted perversion of a man without scruples or honor. I doubt that anyone will hang Bryce Tremayne upside down from a lamppost but maybe they should.

I get to my feet. "I think we're done here," I say.

"Yes, I believe we are," Tremayne says. He doesn't rise from his chair. "Goodbye, Mr. Bernardi. I'm sure you can find your own way out."

I can and I do.

As I stride down the corridor toward the elevator well, I hear someone behind me call my name. I turn as the pudgy boozer with the blonde curls catches up with me. He manages a smile as he thrusts out a chubby hand. "Sorry we weren't introduced. Hubbell Cox. I'm Bryce's p.r. man."

We shake. His hand is not only pudgy, it's sweaty. On his pinky he wears a gold ring with a huge multifaceted emerald. Whatever or whoever Cox is, he isn't poor.

"Sometimes Bryce forgets the amenities," he says apologetically. Like Tremayne he sounds very much a Texan but with a patina of breeding.

I nod. "He seems the type." I push the elevator down button.

"I couldn't let you leave without making sure you understood the extent of Bryce's power and influence," Cox says.

"I'm not dense and your boss isn't subtle," I say. "I got the message."

"I hope so. Bryce can whip his weight in wildcats , no

question, Mr. Bernardi, but even when he's wrong, he can be mighty dangerous and vindictive. Perhaps even more so."

"I sensed that as well."

The elevator arrives. I step in. Cox steps in with me. I tell the operator the lobby. Like or not, Cox is coming with me.

"Do you know Roy Kravitz?" he asks.

I search my brain. "Screenwriter. Pretty good one,too. I think he got an Oscar nod."

"Two," Cox says. "He flew to Zurich a couple of weeks ago. He's taking up permanent residence."

"Looking for excitement, is he?" I say.

Cox ignores me. "Late last month Bryce devoted an entire column to Mr. Kravitz, his history, his friends and acquaintances, his political leanings, then and now. The column suggested that HUAC might have a lot to learn from Mr Kravitz. The next day Kravitz flew to Switzerland."

"Lovely. No trial, no evidence, no witnesses. Just the ravings of a blowhard with a typewriter. Somebody really ought to kill the son of a bitch."

"You will continue to think that way at your own peril, Mr. Bernardi," Cox says.

"Really? Is that some kind of threat?"

"Not at all. Just a warning." He spreads his arms helplessly."I am an object lesson as to what happens when such a warning is ignored."

He looks into my eyes and his gaze doesn't falter. This is a brave and unusual admission coming from an obvious lackey.

"Perhaps you and I should sit down and talk sometime," I suggest.

"Perhaps not," Cox says. "Do you know the best way to handle a raging out of control forest fire, Mr. Bernardi?"

"Other than to spit on it?"

"You start a backfire," Cox says.

"Are you trying to tell me something, Mr. Cox?" I ask.

He smiles as we reach the ground floor and the elevator doors open. "I wouldn't presume, Mr. Bernardi," he says.

I've stepped into the lobby. As I look back, the door is closing and Hubbell Cox, still smiling, is returning to the lion's den. I now have a clue as to why Cox drinks as much as he does, but I wonder why he doesn't just walk away. Maybe it has something to do with the skinny redhead wearing the coke bottle glasses. This is just the first of many questions I am going to have about both Bryce Tremayne and Hubbell Cox in the days to come.

CHAPTER FIVE

he first thing in the morning, I do what I should have done the day before when I walked into Bryce Tremayne's suite unarmed and ill prepared. Instead of driving to the office I head over the hill to the L.A. Times and settle down in front of a microfiche reader to learn what I can about the fascist corn pone from San Antone.

Sweet little white haired Harriet, who knows everything about the morgue files, has supplied me with an index to quickly find what I'm looking for. She's also brought me a cup of coffee and if I asked for it, I'm sure she would supply me with a pillow which I probably will need in an hour or so. The newspaper seems to be up to its eyeballs in straight backed wooden chairs designed, no doubt, by a descendant of Torquemada. In return for all this attention, I feed Harriet's habit which is collecting autographed eight by ten glossies signed "To Harriet" by some of Warners' biggest stars. Today she's looking for Doris Day which will be no problem. Doris is so nice she'll probably actually sign it herself instead of leaving it to her secretary or to me. Harriet is a gem to be prized. I vow never to disappoint her.

The amount of coverage on Bryce Tremayne is staggering though much of it consists of his columns which appear twice a week all across the country in the Hearst papers as well as dozens of independents. Still there's a pile of other stuff as well.

He was born in 1903 in Robert Lee, Texas, youngest of five brothers born to Haskell and Maddie Tremayne. He cut hair. She taught school. At age 15 Bryce was too young to be drafted so he stayed home while his older brothers tagged along after Black Jack Pershing to kick the Kaiser's ass. After the Armistice was signed. his eldest brother Jim Bob came home to a hero's welcome. Harry and Luke stayed behind in Flanders Field. Most of Joshua came back to Robert Lee, all but his right arm. He'd been playing piano with a small combo before he enlisted. No more.

And then I stumble upon an interesting profile on Tremayne which I start reading and am so fascinated I cannot stop. It is slanted, no doubt. You could even call it a hatchet job but my gut tells me the material is basically true. Tremayne, the man, is coming into focus.

He'd worked his way through Baylor and caught on after graduation as a gofer and speechwriter for a San Angelo councilman. When the speeches proved insufficiently persuasive to return the councilman for a second term, Tremayne drifted from job to job before catching on with a third term U.S. Congressman named Artemis Brown. Brown was a man of firm opinions. He loved America, hated nigras and despised lazy good for nothing Mexicans. He kept this last opinion to himself as his district included a couple of thousand Hispanics who were also voting age citizens.

Brown apparently developed a real affection for his firebrand acolyte and he began teaching Tremayne all the things that had made Brown a success, chief of which was learning how to hate and how to make the best use of it. Tremayne started writing letters to the editor lauding Congressman Brown and got the majority of them printed in the small weekly and daily papers throughout the district. Naturally he didn't use his own name but the editors didn't care. They were well written, well thought out and the opinions jibed perfectly with the political philosophies of the various editors and publishers. He never took a shot at the big time which was the San Antonio Express News, maybe out of fear of failure, but he needn't have worried. One of the Express News editors, who kept track of such things, had begun following his contributions undeterred by the various phony names being put forth. The writing style was singular and it belonged to Artemis Brown's boy, Bryce Tremayne, no doubt about it.

The year was 1929 and Brown was in his fifth term, heavily invested in the stock market. His portfolio was worth in excess of two million dollars which proved that even a nobody Congressman in a nowhere district could still steal a hell of a lot of money if he worked it right. And Brown had worked it right. He was leveraged to the hilt and if all went well, he'd be into his third million before the end of the decade. Then came October and Wall Street started to bleed and by the time it was over Artemis Brown had little left except for his mortgaged home, his Congressional salary, and a demanding and pampered wife who was still living in the heyday of the early Twenties. He could have started to rebuild. He still knew how to steal but the fight was gone from him and besides, his favorite pigeons were now as broke as he was. His world, once so bright and gay, had turned grey and ugly. Born poor, he decided to die poor, put a gun to his head and pulled the trigger.

The Republican machine mourned for a day or two and then came to Tremayne and asked him to run for the now vacated seat in Congress. Tremayne jumped at it but he quickly realized that he despised campaigning. He was forced to talk to people, to shake greasy hands, to explain himself and his positions, to display himself at humiliating events like bake sales and fashion shows. In the end the people saw through him. For the first time in three decades a Democrat won the district and in the process, Bryce Tremayne learned a valuable lesson. He loved his country but not the people in it.

Now unemployed and without prospects at a time when work was hard to come by, the editor from the Express News came to his rescue by offering him a job on the paper covering the political news and writing an opinion piece once each week for the Sunday edition. He grabbed the opportunity, vowing never to let it go and he never did.

It was around this time that Bryce met Elvira , only daughter of cattle baron J. Farrell Tompkins whose Jasmine ranch a few miles south of San Antonio encompassed over fifteen thousand acres. She was captivated by Bryce from the start but whether he shared her feelings is open to debate. However, Tompkins was rich which meant that one day Elvira was going to be rich and by now, Bryce Tremayne was tired of being poor. They were married in a lavish ceremony in San Antonio's biggest cathedral. He was 28, cynical and worldly. She was 20, trusting and unworldly.

Two bishops and the parish priest officiated. The Archbishop of the Diocese who was Hispanic was permitted to attend. The governor of Texas and his wife were seated in the second row. The state's two Senators were seated a couple of rows further back. At the hotel reception two hundred and thirty two guests were treated to a barbecue feast, sixteen varieties of wine, a dozen types of liquor including moonshine and a wedding cake that stood six and a half feet tall. Guy Lombardo and his Royal

Canadians supplied the music. Following the reception the freshly minted couple boarded a plane that flew them to the Bahamas for a two week honeymoon at a lavish resort. The first night there Bryce Tremayne was seen playing chemin de fer until the wee hours of the morning. There was apparently no sign of Mrs. Tremayne.

When the happy couple returned from their honeymoon friends were sad to see that Elvira had suffered a broken arm when she slipped and fell on a pier at the marina. Several months later she was admitted to the hospital after she fell on the stairs to the basement and suffered a mild concussion. The next year she had lacerations on her face after falling from a step ladder while arranging glassware in an antique breakfront. At this point she received a visit from her father and it is rumored that he delivered an ultimatum. Divorce Tremayne or be disinherited. She refused and it was only after receiving assurances from Tremayne personally that there would be no more "accidents" that J. Farrell Tompkins returned to the Jasmine ranch.

Soon after the 1932 elections, Tremayne began to focus his anger and disenchantment on the socialist policies of the Roosevelt administration. Republicans in Washington fed him information on a daily basis, knowing he would make good use of it. His columns became more and more popular and finally the edict came down from Hearst himself. Tremayne was to write two weekly columns as well as a major column for the Sunday edition. His columns would appear in every Hearst newspaper across the country. In Hearst's opinion, Bryce Tremayne needed to be read by every right thinking citizen in America. He, above all others, held out hope that some day soon, the madness that was Washington would be stopped and reason returned to a troubled nation.

I sit back in my chair. My butt is aching and I really wish I had a pillow. I'm now positive that the Times buys its furniture at garage sales. I drain the dregs of my cold coffee and contemplate what I have learned. It's a lot and none of it is pleasant. Tremayne is exactly what he appears to be, a power driven megalomaniac who takes joy in destroying the lives of others. On a hunch I search further looking for the name Hubbell Cox. When I find it, Cox is the sole subject of a vicious column accusing him of war profiteering. If what I read is true Cox is Satan incarnate. How odd that Tremayne has put the Devil on his payroll.

I search further and find the column dealing with the screenwriter, Roy Kravitz. It is short on hyperbole and long on facts. Names, dates, quotes from correspondence, official police records, supposedly confidential FBI reports. Kravtiz has been skewered like a barbecued pig. No wonder he ran off to Switzerland. If Tremayne has anything even approaching this level of information on Kazan, the man and the studio and the picture are all in deep trouble.

I copy much of what I have read and then take my leave, profusely thanking Harriet for all her help. Doris's picture will be in the mail by day's end. Harriet gushes in gratitude. She gives so much and asks so little. I decide to send along a dozen roses with the photo.

Before I leave the building I detour by way of Phineas Ogilvy's office. He's on the phone but when he sees me, he finds an excuse to hang up quickly. He looks better. Not good but better. I tell him I have identified the gorilla who punched him around in case he wants to press charges. He seems to perk up a little until I mention Bryce Tremayne. He slumps back in his chair. No, he'll let it go. Too much bother. He hasn't the time. I look him in the eye and he looks away and I realize that he is afraid. Phineas, who I believed was not afraid of anything, wants nothing to do with Bryce Tremayne. I call him on it. He denies it but we both know he's lying. If my intrepid friend won't stand up to this man, who will?

Back at the studio, my number one priority is finding Kazan. I put Glenda Mae on it and fifteen minutes later she tells me that Kazan is down at the costume department with Marlon Brando going over Brando's wardrobe for the film.

I've never met Brando but I've read enough about him to know that he is outspoken and very much his own man. Kazan and I have met peripherally but haven't spoken at length. Nonetheless, Kazan greets me warmly and immediately introduces me to Brando who is wearing a torn tee shirt.

"Nice to meet you," Brando says, "but just so you know, I don't go for that fan magazine stuff." I love a guy who gets right to the point.

"I agree," I say, "and if it wasn't for my job, I'd never go near them."

"Yeah, right. Well, that's good," he says. "And also, I don't want to be fixed up by you guys with any dates or anything, or read in the paper how I'm going out with this one or that one. I mean, no offense, but I got a good idea how you guys operate and I don't want any part of it, no sir."

Kazan jumps in. "Take it easy, Bud. I know a little about how Joe works. Whatever way you want things handled, that's what he'll do. Right, Joe?"

"Right," I say. Bud is Brando's nickname. Only strangers call him Marlon.

"Well, that's good," Brando says. "Very good." And then, as if I wasn't there, he again starts thinking about his tee shirt. "I think maybe we oughta have this tear on the other sleeve and I also think it should go all the way down to here. What do you think about that, Gadge?" he says to Kazan.

Kazan shrugs. "Whatever you think, Bud. You're the one wearing it."

Brando nods. "Yeah, that's right," he mumbles. He turns and walks to a floor length mirror and assesses the effect.

I turn to Kazan. "You and I have to talk. Now," I say quietly. He nods and turns to Brando. "Pick out what you like, Bud. I'll check with you later."

"You got it. Later. Not a problem, man," he says, still looking in the mirror.

Kazan and I walk out into the sunlight. It's a beautiful day. A day for swimming at the beach or hiking in the woods or just laying in a hammock in your backyard sopping up the sun. It is not a day for dealing with Bryce Tremayne.

We stroll slowly toward the back lot and I tell him about my meeting with Tremayne. If he is worried or upset, he doesn't show it. We are passing Stage 7 where they are shooting 'Force of Arms' with Bill Holden and Nancy Olson. Kazan says he's thirsty so we grab a couple of sodas from craft services and find a place to sit down.

"Look, Joe," Kazan says, "I understand your concern but don't worry. I can handle myself and I'm certainly not concerned about a bigoted gas bag like Bryce Tremayne."

"Maybe you should be," I say. "He's out to destroy you any way he can."

"Well, he can't. First of all, I've done nothing wrong and secondly I am no martyr. Politically I know very little about that era but the little I do know I will share with the committee."

"You'll name names then?"

He shakes his head in disgust. "Names. It's a farce. The

names I will give them they already have but when I give them what they already have, they are happy. Another blow has been struck for the American way. Madness, Joe. Simple madness." He falls silent for a moment or two, staring off into space. "What am I supposed to do, raise my fist in defiance like Trumbo and Gardner and the rest of the Ten? Go to prison for what? A gesture? A principle? There is no principle here. I despise what those men are doing. I absolutely do but they have the power and I am not going to throw away my life and my career for a gesture."

"Then you have nothing to hide," I say.

"No more than anyone else from those times who became curious but then walked away."

"And there's nothing substantive which Tremayne could reveal."

"Nothing that I won't be revealing to the committee," Kazan says.

I shake my head. "He seems so sure."

Kazan smiles. "Joe, you worry too much. Guys like Tremayne look at a rainbow and tell you it's red. Sure, it's red but it's also seven other colors.The truth, the whole truth and nothing but the truth, the man has no idea what that means and that's his fatal flaw." He puts his hand on my knee and squeezes it. "I'll be fine," he says and he means it. But because I have seen the workings of my government through four years of war I remain unconvinced.

CHAPTER SIX

harlie Berger isn't mad, he's just annoyed. He keeps dunking his tea bag up and down in the cup but it still isn't the right color. On his desk is the early morning edition of the San Francisco Chronicle. He has folded it open to Tremayne's column and I nonchalantly try to read the headline upside down. The subject matter appears to be Dean Acheson, the Secretary of State, and not Elia Kazan. That's a relief.

"I get this call first thing in the morning," Charlie is saying. "Nine o'clock sharp and since my secretary is unfamiliar with a nine to five workday, I have to answer the damned phone myself." He scowls. "What the hell's the matter with this teabag," he mutters. Dunk, dunk, dunk. "Anyway here's this guy on the other end. Cox, I think he said his name was. He tells me that Mr. Tremayne's meeting with my representative was most unsatisfactory."

"Me being that representative," I say.

"Exactly. He accused you of being uncooperative and coming in with preconceived notions."

I laugh. "He actually said that? That I was the one with the preconceived notions?"

"Hard to figure, isn't it?" Charlie says. He takes a sip of

his tea which is now the color of a football and makes a face. "Jesus," he says. "Now it's ice cold." He shoves it away in annoyance.

"How about if I ask Glenda Mae to make you a cup?" I say. He shakes his head. "Forget it."

I point to the paper. "Well, I guess the good news is that Kazan is not the topic of the day."

He smiles. "You think not?" He picks up the paper and tosses it to me. "Last paragraph," he says.

I look to the bottom of the column. Tremayne's added a p.s.

For all you movie lovers out there, you're in for a real treat on Sunday when I give you the down and dirty on one of America's so-called film icons. That's right. chillun, Uncle Bryce is going to tell you all about Mr. Elia Kazan who, given his druthers, would rather be Red than dead. The boys at HUAC have him in their sights and so do I. Right now Mr. Pinko Kazan is over at Warner Brothers prepping one of Tennessee "Homo" Williams' less savory efforts, "A Streetcar Named Desire." Hard to believe that only six years ago the man brought us "A Tree Grows in Brooklyn" but I guess six years in the city of the Godless has given him the courage to show his true colors. A stooge from Warners came to see me the other day to assure me that I was totally wrong about Mr. Kazan. The stooge lied, of course, but that's what he's paid to do. They call it public relations. Nice try, slick, but I know better. And come Sunday, so will you.

I drop the newspaper back on Charlie's desk.

"Maybe you should have a go at him, Charlie," I say.

"No, thanks, slick," he smiles. "I'm sure you did just fine."

"Jack's not going to be happy," I say.

"Jack's never happy," Charlie says. "He likes it that way."

"Any ideas on how to shut this guy up?" I ask.

"Aside from a Browning automatic rifle, not really," Charlie says.

"You know Cox said something odd to me when I left him the other day and I think he was trying to be helpful. He said the way to control a raging forest fire is to start a backfire."

Charlie shrugs. "Sounds good but I think if there was some dirt to be gotten on Tremayne, somebody would have found it by now. Besides, we're out of time. What are you going to learn in three days?"

"Well stated," I say.

"Well, I'm not a dunce, you know, Joe."

"Never thought you were."

"I'm well read and I know which fork to use when at a dinner party."

"No quarrel here."

"Did you know that I went to public school?"

"I never would have guessed," I say.

"We both know that a decent education doesn't have to cost nineteen hundred fucking dollars a year and especially not for a first-grader. Your kids' world is not necessarily better off by forcing them to hob-nob with a bunch of hoity-toity little brats from the flatlands of Beverly Hills."

Charlie is really getting wound up. I just smile and listen.

"Not every six year old is required to have a wardrobe of hundred dollar dresses just to walk up to a blackboard and spell C-A-T."

"I wouldn't think so," I say.

He holds up two fingers.

"Times two," he says.,

"Times two," I repeat, "Wow. Ugly."

"You bet," he says.

"Is there anything I can do?" I ask solicitously.

"Yeah," he growls. "Get that son of bitch Tremayne out of what's left of my hair."

I head back toward my office bristling a little at Tremayne's characterization of me. I've been called a lot of things but this is the first time for 'stooge'. I'd really like to rub Tremayne's face in a Texas-sized cow patty but I frankly don't have the energy. I've done my best. Now he's Kazan's problem. If I never see the man again that will be just fine.

I smile a hello at Glenda Mae as I enter the office. No phone calls and not much mail. I settle in behind my desk where Glenda Mae has laid out the trades and the L.A. Times. I have two letters. I don't recognize the names of the senders but they're marked 'Personal' so Glenda Mae left them alone. As I tear open the first one and start to read , Glenda Mae brings me my morning coffee. The letter's from a Mrs. Halstead of Newport News, Virginia, who just loved my book. She wept when Walt laid Stella's body on the bed and softly started croon an Irish lullaby. She wonders when I am going to write another book. So do I.

I look up from the letter and Glenda Mae has seated herself in my guest chair, eyeing me patiently. This is odd. Glenda Mae never lingers unless she asks or is asked to.

"Something wrong?" I ask.

"With me? No," she says.

"What?"

"Can you spare a few minutes today? Somebody wants to talk to you."

"Who? What about?" I ask.

"Annie Petrakis. She's in makeup. Right now she's doing Nancy Olson for 'Force of Arms' but she could sneak away."

"And why would I want to talk to Annie Petrakis?" I ask.

"Because until two weeks ago she was living with Roy Kravitz and tomorrow she's going to be out on the street."

"Not married," I say.

"No, but they'd been together nearly four years."

"And after four years he ran off and left her flat."

"He had to."

I mull this over. Damn it, I think. None of this is my business. Why can't everyone just leave me be?

"Tell her to come by any time before lunch," I say. Some guys get led around by their peckers. Me? It's curiosity that someday will get me killed.

"Thanks, boss," Glenda Mae smiles, heading for the door. "I told her you were a good guy."

Annie Petrakis is no beauty but there's a sturdiness to her and I sense deep waters. Dark hair, olive skin, black eyebrows that compliment her chiseled features. As you would expect, her makeup is impeccable and you could almost call her attractive. I put her age at 30 but she could easily be 40.

"Thank you for seeing me. I know you are busy," she says.

"Not that busy. How can I help you?" I ask.

"You met with this Bryce Tremayne?"

"I did."

"I would like you to introduce me," she says.

"What for?"

"I want to set the record straight. About Roy."

"In his eyes, Miss Petrakis, the record is straight," I say.

"But the newspaper story, it was filled with lies."

"I don't doubt it."

She shakes her head. "But how can he do that? Aren't there laws?"

"Sure, but most of the time, they don't apply to men like Bryce Tremayne. They make up their own laws."

She nods and looks away. "Yes. That's what Roy said. I told him he had to fight this man but he just shook his head. He wasn't strong enough or rich enough. He said men like Tremayne always win."

She's strong, I can tell by looking at her, but she's not strong now and I think maybe she's going to lose it.

"Can I get you something?" I ask. "Coffee? A soft drink?"

She just shakes her head.

"Tell me about Roy," I say.

She smiles. "I could talk about him all day," she says, " but that is not what you want to hear. You want to know if he is a Communist. You want to know if this Bryce Tremayne is right about him and I tell you now, Mr. Bernardi, on the life of my father, what he has written are lies."

"Because Roy told you they were lies?" I ask.

"Yes. And because I believe him. He does not lie to me. Ever."

I smile at her. "You are a very loyal and remarkable woman," I say.

"Glenda Mae tells me you have a copy of the article," she says looking over at the pile of Times research on my desk.

"Yes, I do."

"Tremayne claims that on September 21, 1938, Roy attended a Communist cell meeting at the house of a party worker, Edvard Brunson. During the month of September that year Roy was in London working on a screenplay for Alexander Korda. He stayed at the Savoy. Both Korda and the hotel will verify."

I frown. "Might just be a mistake in dates----"

"He claims that on the following January 4, Roy met with Harry Steinman, a union organizer in the garment district and a known cell leader.It could not have happened. Steinman died of heart attack at his home in Queens the day after Christmas. I'm sure there's a newspaper obituary as well as a death certificate. Tremayne says that when the Japanese attacked Pearl Harbor, Roy refused to enlist and spent the entire war dodging the draft. Another lie. They refused to take him even though he volunteered for desk duty. In 1936 Roy contracted frostbite attempting to climb Mt. Whitney and lost half of his left foot. Ever since then he has been wearing special orthopedic shoes. Shall I go on, Mr. Bernardi?"

"Not necessary, Miss Petrakis," I say grimly.

"Maybe if I confront this man with his lies, he will retract his accusations and apologize so that Roy can come home."

"No, he won't," I say, "and you don't have the power to force him to do it. Yes, Roy could sue for libel if he could find a lawyer brave enough to take on the Hearst empire and if he had the tens of thousands of dollars and the months and years it would take to get into court, all the time being unable to work because of the blacklist. Meanwhile the Man gets to sit in his suite at the Biltmore as privileged as the kings of old, protected by moats and modern day knights packing police specials. Is it right? Is it fair? No and no. But it's the way it is. I'm sorry."

She nods sadly. "I, too, am sorry."

"Glenda Mae says you are about to be put out on the street."

She laughs. "Glenda Mae says things like that to get your attention. I have a good friend who will let me move in with her."

"Why don't you just hop a plane and join Roy in Switzerland?"

"Because I have a contract with the studio, Mr. Bernardi, and I honor my obligations. But perhaps more importantly, my father is living in a rest home for the elderly. He is nearly 90 and needs constant care and I am all that is left of his family. I visit him three times a week and I will not abandon him."

I nod. Tremayne has worked his evil well on these people.

They have been crushed and there is nothing anyone can do about it. As Annie is leaving I hand her my business card. I've written my home phone on the back. I tell her she is free to call me any time, day or night. If I can help her I will. I also tell her I will take one major swing at Tremayne about the column. It will do no good. He will laugh at me contemptuously but still I will try because I want the son of a bitch to know that I am onto him. I promise myself I'll get to it right after lunch. Meanwhile I have Warner Brothers work that needs doing. I pick up the second letter marked personal. The message is short and sweet and unsigned. "Who the hell ever told you you could write????" My fans. What would I ever do without them?

It's Friday and we start filming on Tuesday and I have yet to speak with Vivien Leigh. She was in and out of wardrobe a couple of weeks ago but we never connected and for the past few days I have been unable to reach her. She and her husband Larry Olivier have taken a bungalow at the Beverly Hills Hotel but whenever I call she is not there. I leave my name. I never get a call back. I'm getting annoyed. This is not a critical situation but I would like to touch base if only as a courtesy. Also I need to know the do's and don't's of her personal publicity. It's well known that she is difficult to work with. It's less well known that she may be manic-depressive and frequently displays manifestations of clinical mental illness. It's also been rumored that she is suffering from tuberculosis. That may be just a rumor but one thing is starting to become clear. Dealing with her is not going to be easy.

The Oliviers have cleverly arranged their schedules so that, while Vivien is shooting 'Streetcar', Larry will be over at Paramount filming 'Carrie', based on the Dreiser novel. I wonder if Olivier,too, is missing in action. I call Shelley Weintraub, my counterpart at Paramount, to compare notes.

"Like trying to round up smoke rings," Shelley laughs when I tell him my problem. "I've talked to the guy exactly once for a period of six and a half minutes. I timed him."

"Maybe they hate publicity," I say.

"Are you kidding? Does a Ford V8 hate gasoline? They thrive on it. Or at least the right kind."

"Meaning what, Shelley?"

"Meaning I was getting the same kind of runaround you were so one afternoon I drove over to the hotel, maybe to confront the guy and sit him down and get a few things straightened out."

"And?"

"They weren't there but I did talk to a busboy who let me in on a minor bombshell. You paying attention, amigo?"

"All ears," I say.

"Off the record," he says.

"Whatever you say."

"Late afternoon Monday, they're in the Polo Lounge having drinks when all of a sudden Leigh starts raising her voice and then she's yelling at Olivier accusing him of infidelity and yeah, he's trying to deny it and shut her up at the same time but she keeps at it and then she tosses a drink in his face, just like in a bad movie and she runs out of the place and he runs after her. How that never made the papers I'll never know but I gotta tell you, Joe, I think this is what you and I are going to be dealing with for the next few weeks."

"Lucky us," I mutter.

I thank him and hang up. I feel a blue funk coming on. In this corner, Tremayne's crusade to destroy our director, in the other corner, a loopy leading lady and her paranoid delusions. I hope to God my next assignment includes Doris Day and Gordon MacRae. I'm going to need the rest.

I have a quickie lunch at my desk and then at two o'clock I call the Biltmore and ask to speak to Captain America. This time it's a woman who answers the phone.

"Good afternoon. To whom am I speaking?" she says.

"The stooge from Warner Brothers. Who are you?" I ask.

"Jennifer Coughlin," she says.

"You would be the aide de camp to the almighty Captain?" I ask.

"I would," she says.

"I need to speak to him."

"He's not here. Maybe I can help."

"I don't think so."

"Try me," she says.

"His column savaging Roy Kravitz is full of factual errors."

"Is it? I'm shocked," she says. I can hear her smiling.

"Oh, so the Kravitz piece is not an anomaly."

"Hardly."

"Does the Captain do ANY research or does he just guess at everything?"

"A little of this, a little of that."

"Well, I just wanted to warn him that litigation is on the way."

"I doubt it," she says.

"The suit will be instituted by Warner Brothers, not Roy Kravitz. Try doubting that."

"Nice bluff but the studio has no standing on which to file."

"The studio has an as-yet unreleased motion picture written by Mr. Kravitz and the vicious and libelous column will suppress business."

"Prove it," she says.

"Prove it won't," I say.

There is a long silence and then she says, "What are you doing for dinner this evening?"

"I don't know," I say. "Dining with you?"

"If you like eating early. Seven o'clock, Bergin's Horseshoe Tavern. Don't be late."

I'm surprised. "What are you, a native?"

"No. Just Irish."

She hangs up. So do I. I stare at the phone. I wonder what I've let myself in for.

You don't have to be Irish to eat at Tom Bergin's Horseshoe Tavern but it helps. It's not fancy but its predictable and the food is usually pretty good. Located near the Farmer's Market, it's a favorite of locals which is why I am surprised that Tremayne's secretary recommended it. Secretary. Right. She has a name. She told me. What was it? Jenny? That's it. Jennifer. Jennifer what? I kick myself for not remembering. No matter. I think I'll know her when I see her.

I almost don't. My eyes float past her twice before they settle on her. This is the same young woman I saw handing papers to Tremayne, but then again, it isn't. Her hair is down, softly cascading to her shoulders. She's wearing makeup. Not too much. It's just right. And her outfit. What can one say? A tight fitting forest green cashmere sweater and a knee length white pleated skirt. She's an all-round girl who is round in all the right places and I'm not the only one staring at her as she stands near the doorway, scanning the premises in search of yours truly.

I get up from my seat at the bar and walk over to her. I smile at her. She smiles at me. A dozen guys with an O' or a Mac in front of their last names are eating their hearts out. The hostess leads us to a booth in the back and seats us. The jukebox is playing James Melton's version of "Galway Bay" and when I order a couple of Guinesses for me and the lady, I catch myself speaking with a brogue.

The lady known as Jenny giggles. I tell her if she wants a real belly laugh she should see me in a German brauhaus. She giggles again. The Bernardi charm is operating at full tilt.

"By the way," I say, "my name is Joe. And I'm pretty sure yours is Jenny."

"Jennifer Coughlin. Jenny will do," she says.

"And how do you come by knowin' this place, darlin'?" I say. Oops. There's that brogue again.

"My favorite hangout when I was getting my Ph.D from UCLA," she says. "By the way, that's confidential. Bryce thinks I'm a graduate of a secretarial school in Lubbock."

"Really? Secrets from the poobah? This sounds intriguing," I say.

"Not really," she says. The waitress comes to the table. Jenny knows her. They chitchat for a minute or so and then Jenny, without looking at the menu, orders the pot roast with a baked potato and steamed asparagus. I figure she must know something so I hold up two fingers. Jenny gives me a thumbs up as the waitress walks off.

"So, Jenny, at the risk of spoiling this lovely dinner we're treating ourselves to, tell me about Willie," I say

"Willie? What for?"

"Curiosity, mostly. Several nights ago I believe that Willie and that ferret who hangs around with him beat the hell out of a good friend of mine."

"Anything you can prove?"

"Sure, if I can get the two of them into a lineup."

"Which probably isn't going to happen," she says.

"Probably not. You think maybe they were following orders?"

"Willie Babbitt does nothing on his own initiative," Jenny says.

"And the twerp with him?"

"Little Bob Brown does what Willie tells him to do."

I nod. "Is there a Big Bob Brown?" I ask.

"There was," she says.

"Ran up against the wrong guy, I suppose."

"Any guy's the wrong kind of guy when he's carrying a Colt.45." She takes a healthy swig of her Guiness. "So this is it," she asks. "You're going to seduce me by discussing a couple of strong arm men?"

"Not my plan," I say.

"Good, because I know you're much brighter than that. I'm halfway through your novel. I like it a lot."

"Thank you."

"Tell me about yourself," she says. "Not the book-you. The real you."

I'm flattered and the Guiness has loosened me up so I start talking. I give her the down-and-dirty version of my life. The foster home, the Oklahoma oil fields, riding the rails to California where I picked grapes while I went to the local community college. Then the Army when the war broke out. I tell her about Lydia and then about Bunny. I avoid telling her about all the dead bodies I've stumbled over in the past four years. No sense casting a pall on a perfectly lovely evening. By the time I finish we're well into a third Guiness and just starting in on the pot roast.

I make a stab at drawing her out about herself but she parries me deftly.

"Are you serious about the lawsuit?" she asks.

"Absolutely," I lie.

"You haven't a prayer of winning," she says.

"I know," I say. "Is that what we're doing here? Tremayne sent you to call me off?"

She shakes her head. "He doesn't know about this."

"I'd like to believe that," I say.

"Word of honor." She smiles again. It's a hell of a smile. Lewd thoughts are creeping into my brain. "About the lawsuit--," she says.

"We're back to that, eh?"

"I wish you'd reconsider, Joe. As a favor to me."

My invisible antennae pop to attention.

"How so?" I ask cautiously.

She hesitates for a moment. "Can I trust you?" she asks.

"With everything but your virginity," I assure her.

She laughs. "A little late for that." She sips her Guiness. "Can I assume that you want to bring down Bryce Tremayne and everything he stands for?"

I nod. "And that's only for starters."

Good. I get another smile.

"I'm working on a book, Joe. It's about half finished. When it's published, and it WILL be published, Bryce Tremayne will be a footnote on the page marked 'Once Somebodies, Now Nobodies'."

"Let me guess. Your Ph.D. It's in Journalism."

"It is."

"And you've got some kind of handshake agreement with some publisher who shares your view of Tremayne."

"Well put."

"And if Warners on Kravitz's behalf were to institute a lawsuit, it would muddy the waters vis a vis the contents of your book."

"Three for three," she says.

"Where's my kewpie doll?" I ask.

She smiles again. "Don't have one. Will I do?"

Oh, my. Only a blind man who also cannot hear could miss this invitation. A vision of Bunny fills my brain. Bunny is not smiling. Far from it. I am groping for a reply when our waitress returns to the table and whispers something in Jenny's ear. She frowns and then says to me, "Will you excuse me for a moment?"

She gets up and walks to the bar where the bartender hands her the phone. She listens and then talks. The conversation is low volume but animated. After a few more moments she hands the phone back and returns to the table.

"Sorry," she says. "The poobah has summoned me."

I check my watch. Ten after eight.

"At this hour on a Friday night?"

"Twenty four hours a day, Joe. It comes with the job."

She grabs her purse while I toss a twenty on the table and then escort her to the door.

"Can I drive you somewhere?" I offer.

She looks outside and shakes her head. "There's a cab right by the door," she says. She leans forward and kisses me gently on the lips. "Let me know whenever you want to claim that kewpie doll," she says. And then she's out the door and into the cab.

I step outside and watch it feed into traffic and disappear. As I turn to go back into the restaurant, my eye is caught by a familiar figure across the street. Treymayne's pet gorilla Willie is leaning against a maroon Pontiac sedan. He, too, is watching Jennifer meld into the traffic. He starts to open the car door when our eyes meet. He pauses momentarily, giving me a hard look, and then he slips behind the wheel, does a U-turn across oncoming traffic and lights out in pursuit of Jenny's taxi.

Up until this evening I thought my life had turned upside down. Now I realize it has also turned sideways and inside out.

CHAPTER SEVEN

This is the third time Lovsky has jammed an elbow in my ribs and I am getting damned tired of it. The only consolation is that the first two times I made the lay up anyway. This one I miss but I'm not going to take a swing at the guy. He's six-one, probably weights two-sixty , most of it centered in his humungous gut and I think if he sat on me, he'd kill me. I am also on good behavior because if we start any kind of ruckus, the YMCA will eject us immediately from the basketball court, no questions asked and no excuses accepted. And besides, I know Lovsky doesn't mean it, he's just a big clumsy doofus.

I look at Ray who just raises his eyes to heaven. Basketball without a referee can be trying on everybody but mostly we muddle through without lasting anger. Ray Giordano is a lawyer.(My personal lawyer when I need one which is much too often for comfort.) We also have two agents, a choreographer, a copywriter, an actor, a CPA, and a bunch of unemployed guys living at home with their parents. None of us are basketball players. Not even close. Two baskets in a row is a streak. But we have been playing this Saturday game for a couple of years and what we lack in skill, we make up for in camaraderie and post-game beer drinking.

The other guys score and one of them yells "Half!" and we all head for the water cooler. We've been at it for nearly thirty minutes and we are gasping for air like beached whales. I think the score is 18-14 but I'm not sure and I'm also not sure who's winning. I suppose I could take up a gentleman's game like golf or even tennis but I doubt that a lesser regimen would satisfy the Alpha Male in me. At least that's what I tell myself.

I wipe off with a towel and sit on the floor next to Ray, back against the wall. In a few minutes we'll go at it again and then when everyone's good and thirsty, somebody will yell "Game!" and we'll head for Otto's at the end of the block. Losers buy the first round.

I look across the court and two guys walk in. They're wearing dark suits and black patent leather shoes and though I can't see through gabardine, it's my hunch they are also wearing shoulder holsters. It's a sure bet they didn't come to join the game.

The shorter of the two yells out my name. "Bernardi! Anybody here named Bernardi?"

I look at Ray. Ray looks at me. My expression probably says it all. Now what? Stiffly I get to my feet. Shorty sees me and starts over, oblivious to the fact that he is marring the hardwood floor with his sensible shoes.

"You Bernardi?" Shorty asks.

"I am. Who are you?"

He takes out his little leather badge holder, flips it open and shoves it front of my face, an inch from my nose.

"Come with us," he says.

"Where? What for?" I ask.

"The lieutenant wants to see you."

"What lieutenant? See me about what?"

Shorty's getting peeved. "Just come with us, sir, and don't give us any trouble."

"You know it wouldn't hurt to throw an 'Excuse me' or a 'Please' in there somewhere."

"What are you, some kind of wise guy?" Shorty asks.

"No, just an ordinary tax paying citizen who would like to be treated with a little courtesy and respect. Maybe I should contact my lawyer," I say.

Now Shorty is really annoyed. "And why would you want to do that?" he asks, sticking his face very close to mine.

"I don't know. Self protection, maybe. Ray?"

Ray has remained seated, watching all of this with amusement. Now he gets to his feet. "I'm Mr. Bernardi's attorney," he says. "What's the beef?"

The two cops look at each other. Shorty mutters "Jesus" under his breath and then looks back at me.

"Here's what it is, Mr. Bernardi," he says very slowly, articulating every syllable. "Lieutenant Overton has ordered me to find you and bring you to the Van Nuys Division station. Exactly why I do not know but I do know that Lieutenant Overton is assigned to homicide and is a very important personage at headquarters downtown so I do not ask why and therefore I do not expect you to ask ME why."

"Homicide?"

"Homicide," he says.

I nod. "Why didn't you say so?"

Ray and I shower and dress quickly and thirty minutes later we find ourselves in a nicely appointed office at the Van Nuys station. The desk plaque reads Captain W.W. Reilly, Division Commander but the guy sitting across from us is Lieutenant Lloyd Overton who has bounced Reilly from his digs. Therefore I assume Overton has plenty of clout and this matter is relatively important. Ray agrees.

He's a pleasant looking guy, tallish but he tends to stoop and when he walked in, he was aided by a cane. His limp is minor but it's there. He has a full head of ash blonde hair and a neatly trimmed blonde mustache and he wears horn-rimmed bifocals. He rummages around through some papers on his desk and then looks at Ray,

"So, Mr. Bernardi----"

Ray silently jabs a finger in my direction.

"Oh. Sorry. Yes," he says. "Mr. Bernardi, I understand you were acquainted with the newspaper reporter, Bryce Tremayne."

"Were?" I ask.

"Yes. He's dead," he says matter of factly and then hunts for something in his pile of papers.

Ray and I share a look.

"Dead? When? How?" I ask.

"How? Bullet to the brain. When? Don't know exactly. Last night. Early this morning. Medical examiner's working on it. Ah, here we go." He pulls a small scrap of paper from the pile. It looks like a restaurant receipt. He checks the back of it where he has something scribbled. He grunts as he reads it over.

Ray pipes up. "Excuse me, but is my client under suspicion here, Lieutenant?"

"I don't know," Overton says. "Should he be?" He looks up at me. "Wednesday afternoon, you met with Mr. Tremayne at his suite at the Biltmore Hotel."

"I did," I say, "and he was alive when I left."

He looks at me blankly for a moment and then half-smiles. "I see. A joke." The smile fades while he continues to sift through this rat's nest of information. "Your name was in his appointment calendar. Could you tell me what your meeting was about?"

I explain briefly about the column and Kazan. I think he's

listening but I'm not sure. "Very interesting," he says when I am finished, "but I'm not political. Was anyone else there with you while this meeting was taking place?"

I tell him. He nods and scribbles notes on the back of an envelope he's found on the desk.

"Did you make any sort of threats against Mr. Tremayne in front of these witnesses?"

Threats? Witnesses? I look at Ray in a panic.

"Excuse me, Lieutenant, but I think I'm going to have to advise my client not to answer any more questions," Ray says.

Overton looks up with a hurt expression on his face. "I'm sorry. Did I say something to offend you, Mr. Bernardi?"

"You seem to be implying that I had something to do with Mr. Tremayne's death?"

"No, no. I imply no such thing,'" he says. "I'm merely trying to assemble the facts of the case. Could you tell me where you were last night between the hours of, say, eleven o'clock to about five in the morning?"

"What?" I say angrily.

"Now hold on----" Ray interjects.

I override him. "I was home alone, in bed, mostly asleep. I have no corroboration, not even a dog. I did not sneak out of my house and sneak into Tremayne's bedroom and blow his head off with a.45 automatic."

"He didn't die in his hotel suite and the gun was not a.45, more likely a.22."

"Whatever," I growl.

"Lieutenant, is Mr. Bernardi a suspect?"

"Of course not," he says, almost indignantly. "There is someone at your studio that I really need to speak with. He seems to have an excellent motive. A Mr.---- "More rummaging. "Oh, yes, you just told me about him. Mr. Kazan. Yes. Have you any idea how I can get in touch with this man?"

Now I am furious. "No, I don't and if you think that Elia Kazan is responsible for a murder, you are out of your fucking mind. The man is an international celebrity, for God's sake."

Overton looks at me with genuine surprise. "Is that a fact? A celebrity? I never heard of him."

"He's a world famous movie director," I say petulantly.

"Oh, movies." he says. "I never go to movies."

"Well, a lot of people do, Lieutenant," I say, really annoyed by this clueless dolt.

"No doubt," Overton says. "Nonetheless, I will need to speak to him."

I get to my feet. "Am I under arrest?" I ask.

"Of course not," Overton says.

"Then I'm leaving. Let's go, Ray."

Ray gets up. So does Overton.

"Mr. Bernardi, I was hoping for your help in this matter," he says.

"No chance of that, Lieutenant," I say. "Not if you're going to try to hang this on Kazan. And next time you want to talk to me, talk to him." I jab a thumb in Ray's direction. Ray takes out a business card and hands it to Overton with a smile and then we get the hell out of there.

Outside we head for the parking lot where we are parked side by side.

"Weird," I say.

"How do you mean weird?" Ray asks.

"Overton. He's a screwball."

Ray grabs me by the elbow and shakes his head.

"I don't know the guy, Joe," he says, "but I do know of him

and he didn't get to be the number two guy in Homicide by stumbling and bumbling. He may have you in his crosshairs and you'll never know it until the moment they slap the cuffs on."

"You're kidding," I say in disbelief.

"Wish I were. Tread softly, amigo. Keep your eyes wide open and if you think you're being followed you probably are."

I shake my head. "What a way to start the weekend."

Once in my car I don't head for home but drive to the studio. No one's there but that's where my wheeldex is and all the phone numbers I'm going to need over the next hour or so.

My first call is to Charlie at home. He's not there but I get the housekeeper.

"Mr. Berger is at dance class with the little ones."

"Dance class?"

"Yes. They study dancing. How do you say it, ballet?"

"Right. Ballet."

"Then they go to May Company for shopping. Little dancing dresses and shoes." I can see Charlie at rehearsals and recitals chatting with all the other 'mothers'. It's not a pretty sight.

"When will he be back?"

"I don't know, Senor. He did not say. Maybe two, three o'clock."

I ask her to have Charlie call me as soon as he gets in and I hang up. I find my number for Kazan. He's staying at the Chateau Marmont on Sunset Boulevard but there's no answer in his room. There's a chance he's here on the lot going over last minute details so I call Burt Yarrow, the unit production manager. Burt tells me that Kazan's on Stage 17 checking the set or at least he was thirty minutes ago. I tell Burt to get word to him that we have to talk. Don't let him leave.

"Joe, what the hell's going on?" Burt asks.

"About what?" I ask innocently.

"Kazan. A couple of hours ago I get a call from the cops wanting to know where they can find him."

"What did you tell them?"

"I gave them the hotel, what else? I don't screw with cops. Twenty minutes later they call back and say Kazan never showed up at his room last night so is he at the studio? Now I gotta be careful so I say I don't know. And I don't. Not for sure. So, Joe, like I asked before, what's the problem?"

"Its a long story, Burt, but Bryce Tremayne is dead. Somebody killed him."

"Holy crap," Burt says.

"That's all I know. When I get more I'll fill you in. Meanwhile if you find Kazan tell him to sit tight while I try to figure out what to do."

"Will do," he says.

I hang up and I think about calling Jack Warner but something holds me back. He needs to know but do I have to be the one who tells him? If I do, I'll all of a sudden be dealing with studio lawyers and security and at the moment that's something I don't need. I think maybe playing Greek messenger is better left to Charlie.

I have a lot of questions and no answers so I dig out the home number for Aaron Kleinschmidt. He's a Detective Sergeant with the Metro Division and wired in. What he doesn't know he can find out. We're not exactly beer drinking buddies but we're a lot closer than strangers. I call his house. No answer. It's possible though not likely that he's drawn weekend duty. Nonetheless I call Metro and within a minute or two he comes on the line.

"My ex took Josh to San Francisco for a three day holiday so what am I supposed to do? Sit around the house pulling my pud?" he says when I ask how he's doing. Josh is his twelve year old boy. Aaron's a weekend father.

"I need help," I say.

"Christ, Joe, you always need help. What now?"

The first time we met he tried to frame me for a murder I didn't commit. Then he cleaned up his act and the second time, I helped him take credit for solving the killing of a really sleazy Hollywood flesh peddler. That put him on Chief Parker's A-list. He grumbles when I call him but he has a good memory.

"Bryce Tremayne."

"You gotta be kidding. You're involved with that one?"

"Up to my ears."

"Good luck," he says. "You met Overton yet?"

"This morning."

"Watch your step," he says.

"Who is this guy? Why is everybody warning me?"

"You ever hear the one about the wolf in sheep's clothing?"

"Aesop."

"Whoever."

"Tell me about the case. Overton gave me nothing."

"That figures. I don't know much, Joe. but from what I hear around the squad room, I can tell you this. It's big. The victim's a VIP so the pressure's on. Except for Overton, nobody wants any part of this one. It's a no-win career buster."

I'm puzzled. "How so?"

"You really don't know, do you?"

"Know what?"

"Anything."

"I already told you that."

There's a long pause. Then Kleinschmidt says, "Okay, you didn't get this from me. You know the Smoke House restaurant?"

"Sure. It's across the street from the studio."

"Security found the guy behind the wheel of his car when they were making early morning rounds. Probably five-thirty or six. He'd taken one to the head. One shot. Small caliber."

"Okay," I say.

"His pants were down over his knees. So were his skivvies."

I picture it. It's not a pleasant sight.

"He still had his wallet, full of cash and he still had his watch and his diamond pinkie ring."

"Sounds like robbery's not going to fly," I say.

Kleinschmidt continues. "In his shirt pocket they found a pack of matches from the Naked Apollo. You ever hear of the place?"

"I think so," I say. "A hangout for queers?"

"That's it."

"Wow," I say to myself very quietly.

"So, Joe, some of the guys here actually read the papers. They're talking about this guy Tremayne and his column for Sunday where he's going to unload a lot of crap on your director. Except now Tremayne's dead and maybe there isn't going to be any column. And every guy in the room knows that somebody is going to have to question Elia Kazan, the world famous stage and film director, about a dead guy in a parking lot with his pants down and his willie hanging out for all the world to see."

"A career buster."

"You said it," he says.

"Makes you wonder about Overton. doesn't it?"

"Well, you met him. Like I said, a good cop but a little---"

He pauses.

"Vague?" I say.

"I was going to say eccentric," Kleinschmidt says. "Any more questions?"

"Got all I need," I say.

"Good luck." He hesitates. "And, Joe, the homosexual business. All of it's a holdback from the press and the public. You tell no one. Not your lawyer, not your boss, not your gal. It may get out anyway but if I find out it came from you, I don't know you, now or ever again. Understood?"

"Understood," I say.

I start to hang up, then quickly I say, "Wait!"

"What?"

"The matches. Was it a new pack? Used? What?"

"How the hell should I know? Take care, Joe."

He hangs up.

And I'm thinking, if Tremayne doesn't smoke and I know he doesn't, what's he doing with a pack of matches in his pocket?

CHAPTER EIGHT

check with the main gate. Because it's Saturday there have been few cars in and out. As far as the gate guard knows, Kazan is not on the lot because he never appeared this morning. On the other hand, he also hasn't left either. But he is here because Burt Yarrow saw him earlier so now it's a matter of tracking him down.

The studio has assigned four sound stages to 'Streetcar":12, 17, 18 and 21. Kazan also has a private office in one of the production buildings. I check there first. It's dark and locked. I head for Stage 12. Production designer Richard Day and his crew are hard at work. Day says he hasn't seen Kazan, not this morning. I head for 17 and 18 which are side by side. These two are dark except for worklights. I call out Kazan's name. No reply. I'm getting discouraged. I open the door to Stage 21. Same story. Deserted. Work lights. I call out Kazan's name as a formality.

"Yo," I hear from afar.

"Mr. Kazan?" I call out.

"Back here!"

I head for the rear of the stage and find Kazan sitting on a sofa on the set. He has a work light directly overhead and a looseleaf notebook open on his lap. He looks up as I approach.

"Joe? I thought that was your voice. What are you doing here on a Saturday?"

"Looking for you."

"No trouble, I hope." He says it offhandedly still concentrating on his work. He seems to be sketching. "This damned set. We still haven't got it right. I can't put the camera where I want."

I say nothing. He is aware of the silence and he looks up at me. "What?"

"You didn't go back to your hotel last night," I say.

"No, I didn't," he says. "I slept on the sofa in my office. Is that a crime?"

"No, THAT isn't," I say.

He caught my inflection. He closes the notebook and gives me his full attention. "What is it, Joe?"

"Bryce Tremayne is dead."

He frowns, trying to compute it. "Dead. Well, there's a surprise."

"Murdered," I say.

His eyes narrow. "There's a bigger surprise," he says. "How?"

"Shot," I say.

He shakes his head. "Terrible," he murmurs.

"The police are looking for you," I tell him.

He looks genuinely startled by that. "Me? What for?" He mulls it for a moment and then he gets it. "That's absurd," he says testily.

"They have questions. For the moment, that's all it is. They'll want to know where you were last night."

"I'll tell them."

"Can anybody verify it? Security? Cleaning crew? Anything like that?

He shakes his head. "I don't think so." He looks at me and I see worry in his eyes. Not fear. Just a little bit of worry. "Joe, I didn't kill anybody."

"I know that, Mr. Kazan. The idea is ridiculous," I say. "But these guys are cops, not critics. They won't be in awe of your reputation, not if they think you're involved."

He shrugs with a raise of his eyebrows.

"Guess I'm going to need a lawyer," he says.

"Not yet," I say. "We'll see where it goes. If it comes to that, the studio will get you someone."

"Comforting," he says. "And by the way, call me Gadge. Everybody does."

"Sure," I say.

His face is sad and now I see the vulnerability that has been masked by his defiance. "Why won't they listen, Joe? What's the matter with these people whose minds are so closed, people who don't even know me but are able to tell what I think and what I feel. Vivien, with her English sensibility, said it best. I am a victim, scourged by the unkindness of strangers."

"'You're an articulate man, Gadge. You can defend yourself."

He shakes his head with a wry smile. "My friends will defend me regardless and my enemies will revile me no matter what I say. This is just something I will have to live through."

"Hello! Anybody in here?" The voice reverberates through the soundstage. I think I recognize it.

"You ready?" I ask Kazan quietly.

"I suppose I'd better be," he replies.

"Back here!" I call out.

In a few moments, Lieutenant Overton appears accompanied by a uniformed Metro, Jesse Groenwald, the studio's chief of security, and Burt Yarrow. Overton smiles.

"Good afternoon, Mr. Bernardi," he says and then turns to Kazan. "And a good afternoon to you as well, Mr.Kazan. You've been a hard man to track down."

We all walk out into the sunlight. Kazan has refused to accompany Overton to police headquarters but he has volunteered to answer questions in his studio office. No, he doesn't need a lawyer, he says. He has nothing to hide. I take off, hoping to hook up with Charlie Berger so I can unload this mess onto him. If I don't find Charlie I am going to have to notify Jack Warner of the situation. That's not something I am looking forward to.

I go back to my office to make another try at Charlie Berger and this time I get lucky. He has just returned from shopping with his girls. I fill him in and he's as shocked as I am, not only by Tremayne's death which is bad enough but the idea that Kazan might have been involved. Neither of us believe that for an instant but certain factions of the Hollywood press are predatory and thrive on celebrity scandals. He needs to be severed from this mess immediately and cleanly, so cleanly that no one would dare speculate on his involvement.

I tell Charlie that I'm pretty sure I can get Phineas Ogilvy to slant it our way. Phineas is already part of the story courtesy of the roughing up he got from Tremayne's boy, Willie. And Phineas may be able to exert a little pressure on Lou Cioffi, the paper's top crime reporter. Maybe. I promise to get on it right away.

It's only a matter of time before the papers and the radio and TV will have the story so I call Phineas immediately at his home. He's been out on his deck, lolling in a hammock and reading. He's heard nothing and when I tell him the sleazy details he is shocked. Better yet, he,too, is appalled by the idea that anyone in his right mind would think that Kazan is involved. I tell him everything I know including the little I got from Kazan himself. He promises a glowing pro-Kazan column in the morning and will get in touch with Cioffi right away.

I realize there is someone else I need to talk to immediately and I place a call to the Biltmore. I ask for Captain America but am told that there is no one by that name registered at the hotel. I ask for Jennifer Coughlin. No luck. How about Hubbell Cox? Not registered. Sorry. They hang up. Okay, they've either changed the password or skedaddled. This will require an in-person inquiry at the Biltmore because the last time I saw Jenny Coughlin, she was in a cab headed for a rendezvous with a soon-to-be corpse named Bryce Tremayne and being closely followed by Tremayne's muscle man, Willie. In the back of my mind is the comforting notion that if I can lay this murder off on someone else, Kazan and the studio and the film will be free to proceed unencumbered. A little voice in the back of my brain is warning me, "Joe, this is above and beyond your pay grade." I hear it but decide to ignore it.

I hand my car over to a Biltmore parking valet at a few minutes to three. When I step inside the lobby is crowded. The tourists and sightseers are here in droves. Monday through Friday the hotel caters to a business clientele. Come the weekend and we get the gawkers, the ones who roam around Beverly Hills and Brentwood with their movie star maps in one hand and a camera in the other, hoping to get their picture taken with Buster Crabbe.

I head straight for the elevators because I know where I'm going. I get off on the sixth floor and head down the plushly carpeted corridor toward the suite at the far end. I pass a housekeeper and toss her my best bashful 'aw shucks' smile. She smiles back. When I get to the door of 6001 I knock quietly. No response. I knock a little louder. Nothing. I reach for my wallet and take out my newly acquired Diner's Club card. I slip it in the door slot near the lock and pull up. Nothing. I try again, twisting and jiggling the card. I extract the card and look at it. I've badly bent one corner. This is odd. Last year I watched an ex-cop pull this off in less than three seconds. Maybe it's like the trick with the tablecloth and the dishes. Either you know how to do it or you don't.

As I stand there trying to re-bend my card back into shape, I'm suddenly aware of a man standing next to me. He wears an ill-fitting three- piece suit and a.38 police special under his arm. Our eyes meet and for a moment he just stares at me. Then he says with a smile, "Lose your key?"

I look at him and I say, "House dick?"

He nods slowly, still smiling.

His name is Roscoe Heep and he invites me to his office where he sits me down in a chair facing his desk. He asks for my wallet and I give it to him. He's still packing the.38. He goes around his desk and sits, then picks up the phone and dials a number. He reads my information into the phone. After a moment or two, he grunts and hangs up. He hands me back my wallet.

"Why so curious about 6001?" he asks.

"I was there a couple of days ago. There was someone I needed to speak to."

"Captain America?" Heep says with an amused grin on his face.

"No. He's dead," I say.

"I know. It was on the radio a couple of hours ago. So who'd you want to speak to?"

"His secretary. I guess they checked out," I say.

"In a manner of speaking," Heep says. "What'd you want to talk to her about?"

"That's my business," I say.

"I think it's mine," Heep says. "His dying reflects badly on the hotel."

"He didn't die here," I remind him.

"Semantics," he says. "The hotel may be mentioned in the newspaper coverage in an unsavory manner."

"Possibly," I say.

"It's my job to prevent that," he says.

"It's my job to see that our aspiring starlets keep their mouths shut when they get knocked up by one of our dashing leading men. I don't always succeed."

Heep shrugs. "Life sucks."

"Where are they?" I ask.

"Eighth floor under the name John Smith," he says.

"Clever," I say admiringly.

"I tried for Murgatroyd but I couldn't spell it."

"Who can?" I ask. "Why the move?"

"Mostly because of the wife. When she heard her husband was dead, she started screaming. They're going to kill us! They're going to kill us! I have no idea who 'they' are but we had to get the hotel doctor up to the suite to calm her down. We had an empty suite. We moved them. No big deal," he says.

He reaches in the middle drawer of his desk and takes out a photograph. "Since you seem to be all over this case like mud on a pig, maybe you can help me out. Who's this?" he asks as he slides the photo toward me. I look at it. It's been taken from a distance and blown up. It's a woman sitting in a chair in the lobby of the hotel. There is an anxious look on her face. There's no question. It's Annie Petrakis.

I slide the picture back to Heep, shaking my head. "I have no idea. What's her story? Hooker? Pickpocket? Crazy lady?"

"She was trying to get to Tremayne. She tried every trick in the book but my people know better. Then she just sat there, eyes fixed on the elevators, hoping to catch him going out. After a couple of hours I walked over to her and told her to get out or I'd call the cops. She just got up and left without saying a word."

"Strange."

"Even more so now that Tremayne is dead. You're sure you don't know her?"

"No clue. So, Roscoe, that phone call you made when we walked in. Will they see me or won't they?"

"Won't. Sorry, Joe."

I nod. "I get it. I may try to phone them later. Who do I ask for to get through?"

"Try John Smith," he says dryly.

I drive back to the studio. It's now late in the day but there's somebody I need to speak with right away before Overton catches up with her. The trouble is, the studio address for Annie Petrakis is no good. She's just been evicted from her apartment but someone may know where she ended up. I find the number I want in the wheeldex and call. Her husband Beau answers the phone.

"Beau, it's Joe Bernardi."

"Well, Joe, it's sure mighty nice to hear your voice," he says in that lazy Mississippi drawl. "How ya been keepin' yourself, possum?"

"Okay," I say, "but I need to speak to Glenda Mae."

"Just left for the market, Joe. She's fixin' lasagna and ran outta tomatoes. Shouldn't be long. Maybe twenty minutes. Where are you?"

"The office," I say.

"Say, I just recalled that your lady's not in town. How's about comin' by here for supper. Love to have you and I can guarantee the lasagna."

"Darned nice of you, Beau, but I have plans. Maybe some other time. Have Glenda Mae call me when she gets in."

"I surely will," he says.

I hang up. I'm sure the lasagna's heavenly but I had to beg off. I have to stay loose because right now the situation is very fluid.

While I'm waiting for Glenda Mae's call back, I sort through the background material I accumulated at the Times. I'd copied about a dozen of Tremayne's columns that had looked interesting. I pick up the one headlined "Cox Dips His Mitt in the Wrong Cookie Jar". I've read it once. Now I decide to read it much more carefully.

During the war Hubbell Cox owned a factory that manufactured hardware for U.S. Navy fighter planes. Things were lush until war's end when the government started cutting back and terminating contracts. Cox's company was one of those caught in the squeeze. Starting in early 1946 he began dipping into the company's separate retirement fund account in order to keep the doors open. Tremayne called him on it and Cox denied everything, wrapping himself in the American flag and threatening legal action. Apparently Tremayne kept at it and found the goods, spelling it out in language even a moron could understand. Local prosecutors got into it and brought charges but Tremayne's "proof" was not courtroom proof and Cox was never brought to trial, even as his company went bankrupt. In the final paragraph of the column Tremayne labeled Cox a "true American and an unashamed patriot" but also a man who let fear and his own incompetence overwhelm him. In Tremayne's words, he stood as an example to all those rich and powerfully connected men of industry that dishonesty will out and even the most respected individuals must face equal justice under the law.

I have a lot of questions. Too bad Tremayne's not around to answer them. For instance, how did Cox seque from target to employee? Forgiveness? Respect for his skills as a businessman? Or did Cox have some secret sway over Tremayne, information that dare not see the light of day. In the research Cox was described as a 41 year old bachelor. Was that out of choice or was there something inherent in his sexual nature that precluded it. Given the circumstances surrounding Tremayne's death, I think it is a legitimate question.

The phone rings. I pick up. It's Glenda Mae. Before I can get past hello, she's repeating Beau's offer to feed me. Again I demur with reluctance. I ask her if she knows where Annie Petrakis is now staying. She doesn't and says she has no way to find out until Monday morning when she can poke around the makeup department.

I thank her and hang up and then put my head in my hands. I am suddenly very tired. I have been going full bore ever since my return from New York City. I've been eating slop and sleeping badly, determined to protect the reputation of a man who it may turn out had at one time advocated the overthrow of the United States government. I don't know for sure what Elia Kazan stands for or what he stood for in the past and maybe that's my fault because I haven't asked him. Maybe I'll ask him tomorrow or the next day or maybe never but I do know one thing. My adrenalin is gone, I'm dead tired and I just want to go home.

I check my watch. Nearly five o'clock. That makes it nearly

eight in New York. I don't really expect to get a call from Bunny on a Saturday night but you never know. So I go home. I have a can of split pea soup and toast. I eat a stale doughnut for desert and haul out the Coors. I watch an old movie on Saturday Night Theater on Channel 5. Chester Morris has crashed his plane in a South American jungle and is trying desperately to save a bunch of people who don't deserve to be saved. I fall asleep. The phone doesn't wake me but at eleven o'clock my eyes pop open with the test pattern showing on my television screen. I trudge into the bedroom and slip under the covers. I lay very still, staring at the ceiling. And still the phone does not ring.

CHAPTER NINE

I don't usually roll out of bed early on a Sunday morning but today I make an exception. It's quarter of seven. I check the front stoop for my Sunday Times. It hasn't been delivered yet. I go in the kitchen and percolate a pot of coffee. I search for fixings for breakfast. The selection is thin but I do discover an unopened can of corned beef hash in the back of a shelf and one egg remaining in the carton. There's no bread and no juice but what I have will suffice.

I think I hear a clunk at my front door. That would be Jimmy whats-his-name from the next block, my delivery boy, tossing my paper onto the stoop. The kid must be in good shape. Tossing the Sunday Times is no mean feat.

I finish frying up the egg and the hash and set them on the dinette table along with my coffee and go to get the paper. I set it down beside my plate and scan page one. It's all there. No need to look inside.

CELEBRITY MURDER BAFFLES POLICE. That's the headline on the lead story, right hand side above the fold. There's a file photo of Bryce Tremayne and a stock shot of the Smoke House restaurant. Lou Cioffi's byline accompanies the story. I quickly scan the text. The emphasis is on mystery. There are few clues, no witnesses, no apparent motive. Overton has apparently withheld the condition of the victim's trousers and there is no public hint of sexual involvement, hetero or otherwise. The public is asked to cooperate. A phone number for tips is highlighted. Most of these tips will be bogus. A few really demented creatures will appear to confess to the murder. It happens all the time but unless they know about Tremayne's immodesty in death, they will be shooed away like pesky flies.

My eyes fall to the last paragraph and I start to feel relief. It says that famed director Elia Kazan, who has come under fire from Tremayne's columns in recent days, has expressed sympathy to Tremayne's widow. It also says that Kazan spent the entire night on the Warners studio lot, has been cooperating fully with the authorities and has been cleared of any suspicion.

I look to the left of the page where Phineas Ogilvy has written a sidebar to the main story. Always enterprising, Phineas somehow got in touch with the man himself and his column is liberally sprinkled with direct quotes from Kazan expressing horror at the murder and deep sympathy for those Tremayne left behind. Phineas, too, emphasizes the fact that Kazan is not and never was a suspect in this tragic killing.

I scrape off my plate and leave it in the sink, then head off to the bedroom feeling a hundred percent better about the situation. I shave and shower and slip into slacks, a collared shirt and a lightweight cream-colored cotton sweater. I'm ready to head out the door when the phone rings. It's Charlie Berger.

"Nice work, Joe," he says. "The Times story and the piece by Ogilvy, I couldn't have asked for better coverage."

"Don't thank me, Charlie. Thank Phineas. He's the one who got Cioffi to downplay Kazan."

"Whatever," he says. "Now tell me something, Joe. I'm sitting here looking at Tremayne's column in the Herald-Examiner. Wasn't he supposed to be doing a hatchet job on Kazan?"

"That's what he promised at the tail end of his Friday column."

"Guess he changed his mind," Charlie says. "I'm reading this longwinded thing about socialists worming their way into unions in every part of the country and in particular, the Teamsters, who already have the power to shut down the country. Kazan isn't mentioned anywhere."

"Strange," I say.

"Not that I'm complaining," Charlie says. "It just caught me by surprise."

"Me, too, Charlie. I'll look into it."

"Joe, don't look too hard. Tremayne is history. Let's not resurrect him."

"Right, boss. I hear you."

I hang up. Charlie's right. Hunker down. Keep quiet. Let these events fade with time. No one will remember. On the other hand, a man's been murdered and a potentially career killing newspaper column has disappeared. I inwardly cringe at the thought but I can feel curiosity starting to get the better of me.

I call the Biltmore and ask for John Smith. After two rings a woman picks up.

"Daddy?" she says.

"No, this isn't Daddy," I say.

Her voice had been soft and plaintive. Now it's hard and bitchy.

"Who is this?"

"Joe Bernardi from Warner Brorhers and good morning, Mrs. Tremayne. Allow me to express my profound regret at your loss."

"What do you want?" she asks somewhat ungraciously.

"I need to speak to Miss Coughlin," I say.

"She's not taking calls, " Elvira Tremaye says, "and please hang up. I'm expecting an important phone call."

"She is taking calls, Mrs. Tremayne, and if you don't put her on the phone right away, I will be over there in thirty minutes with a couple of reporters, a photographer, and a newsreel crew."

"What did you say your name was?" she asks.

"Q.P. Dahl from Warner Brothers," I tell her.

I hear her put the phone down and a minute later, Jenny comes on the line.

"Nice alias," Jenny says.

"I knew you'd remember," I say. "We'll always have the Horseshoe Tavern."

"If you say so," she says.

"Oh, we're playing that game."

"What game?"

"We have to talk," I say.

"Not possible," she replies.

"Make it possible," I say. "Shake loose from that exhilarating crowd you hang with before I remember how you went tearing away from our dinner date at the behest of your boss only a scant few hours before he was killed."

Silence. Glibness gone. Then she says, "May I assume you haven't shared that fact with the police?"

"Not yet, but my patience is not infinite."

"Where?" she asks.

"The La Brea Tar Pits," I say.

"Where is that?"

"In Hancock Park. I'll meet you by the T-Rex in an hour."

"I still don't know----"

I cut her off. "You'll find it," I say and hang up.

The La Brea tar pits are extraordinary as well as singular. Black primordial tar oozes to the surface now and then exposing the bones of long dead dinosaurs. There is no other place on earth like it, at least not one that I know of. And only in Los Angeles would someone dream of melding prehistoric science with the theatricality of the Ringling Brothers circus. Man made models of every species of dinosaur are scattered throughout the park, some depicted rising from the goo. It is a delightful place to visit if you are prone to sweaty nightmares.

I beat her there by a couple of minutes. The big T is towering over me giving me a chance to admire his perfectly sculpted teeth. He was a flesh-eater and not fussy about the kind of flesh he ate but the Ice Age put an end to that for which I think all us humans should be eternally grateful. As I look past his outstretched paw, I see Jenny approaching from the west entrance. There's something about the way she swings her body that brings out the worst in me. Maybe that's why I insisted on a face to face meeting.

She smiles as she comes near and points to T-Rex.

"Jack Warner?" she asks.

I look up at the beady eyes and the gaping open mouthed grin.

"Distant cousin," I say.

"Nice place you picked for a meet," she says.

"Not nice. Perfect for privacy. My kind of people and your kind of people wouldn't be caught dead in a tourist trap like this."

"Not even to visit the ancestors?" she asks. She smiles. I love that smile.

"Come on, let's walk. I'll buy you a pretzel at that stand over there."

We start to amble. It's a gorgeous day. Not a day for business but I haven't much choice.

"So," I say, "what happened to the column about Elia Kazan?"

"It was decided that running it would be inappropriate."

"Decided by whom?" I ask.

"It was a group decision," she says.

"Was it? Should I poll the jury? How about the skinny red-head with the thick glasses? Does he get a vote?"

She laughs. "Who? Boyd?"

"Is that his name?"

"Boyd Larrabee. He's the bookkeeper."

"Shouldn't he be back in Texas cooking the books?"

"He is. We let him out only when necessary."

I nod. "And what's with him and Hubbell Cox?"

"Oh, you noticed," she said.

"I'm not blind, woman," I say.

"Let's say Hubbell is smitten and Boyd less so. A lot less."

"Unrequited love. I fear an unhappy ending," I say.

"Sooner or later," she says.

We've reached the pretzel vendor. I hold up two fingers. He hands us two nice big hot pretzels. I give him a buck and we keep walking.

"Now, about that fascinating column on labor unions."

"Let's say I made that decision on my own," Jenny says.

"Let's say that."

"We always have a back up column ready to go in case of emergency. I thought this might be a good time to run it."

"And why is that?" I ask.

"The other day on the phone you mentioned the Roy Kravitz column."

"I did."

"I dug out a copy and re-read it. In light if your criticsim, I felt uncomfortable."

"You hadn't researched the piece," I say.

"I don't do research. I'm a secretary. Bryce did his own research."

I nod. "And you felt that if the Kazan piece was equally as inaccurate Bryce would be opening himself up to trouble at precisely the wrong time."

"Yes."

"Besides which, if you could save the Kazan column for dissection in your book, it would make your publisher extremely happy."

Her eyes flicker for just a moment. Then she says, "That, too."

The pretzel has now made me very thirsty so we walk over to the guy selling cold sodas. I opt for a Nehi. She has a Dr. Pepper and we head for a nearby bench.

"When did you pull the switcheroo?" I ask.

"I teletyped the replacement column to the paper early Friday evening, just before I met you for dinner."

"But Bryce must have found out what you'd done and called you at the restaurant."

She nods with an appreciative smile. "That's right though I still can't figure out how he found me."

"He had you followed by Willie Babbitt."

"No."

"Yes. And when you left the Horseshoe in the cab, Willie followed you back to the Biltmore."

She shakes her head. "But I didn't go back to the Biltmore. I met Bryce at Chasen's where he was having dinner."

"Alone?" I ask.

"No. He had someone with him."

"Who?"

"I don't know. There were two places set. They were still on drinks. There was a smoldering cigarette butt in the ashtray. Whoever it was had either gone to the rest room or maybe to make a phone call."

"What did Bryce say to you?"

"He ordered me to retract the backup column and teletype the one on Kazan."

"And?"

"He was drunk and loud and ready to cause a scene. I said I would and got the hell out of there."

"And?"

"Halfway back to the hotel, I changed my mind. The way he was going he'd be falling down drunk by midnight. He wouldn't be in any condition to check on me and if he woke up Saturday morning and decided to fire me, well, so be it. I already had plenty to bury his sorry ass. More than enough."

I nod. "And getting fired, that would also be really great for the book."

I give her my serious, deadpan look. She sees through it and starts to laugh. "That, too," she says. And I start to laugh along with her.

A Mom and Dad come by pushing a baby carriage. An old man comes from the other direction, stooped over and using a cane but his eyes are still bright and he smiles in greeting. I smile back. A little kid comes running toward us carrying a foot high toy stegosaurus out in front of him, grrr-ing at everyone in sight. He grrrs at me. I grrr back. He laughs and keeps running.

I look at Jenny. She's smiling at me.

"Are you spoken for?" she asks.

"In a way," I say. "How about you?"

"No."

"At the risk of offending you," I say, "tell me about your relationship with Tremayne."

"You mean, was I sleeping with him?"

"That's a start."

"No, I wasn't."

"Why? Wasn't he interested?"

She laughs a little. "Oh, he was interested, all right, but before I took the job, I made it clear that my virtue didn't come with the shorthand."

"And still you got the job."

"I did. With a condition. That if people thought we were sleeping together, that I do nothing to discourage the idea."

"Odd," I say.

"Bryce was odd in many ways," she says.

"Homosexual?"

"That's a strange question," she says.

"Actually it's not," I say. I tell her about the condition of Tremayne's body in the car at the restaurant parking lot. She reacts but she's not surprised.

"I was always felt that Bryce was a man of lusty appetites and that the gender of his partner was a secondary consideration."

"Does Hubbell Cox fit into this scenario somewhere?"

She nods her head with an appreciative smile. "You don't miss much, Joe."

I smile back. "Try not to. So, " I say, "you were headed back to the hotel determined to leave the backup column in place. And?"

"And I went up to the suite to see if there were any emergencies that needed handling."

"And were there?"

"No."

"Was Hubbell Cox around?"

"No, but I didn't expect he would be. Hubbell was good at finding diversions , even in strange cities."

I nod. "And the boys? Willie and Little Bob?"

"Probably keeping an eye on Bryce although I didn't see them at the restaurant."

"How about the wife with the freshly minted black eye?"

"Out."

"Unusual?"

"Yes. She hated being out alone."

"What about her Daddy? She was expecting his call. Might he have showed up?"

"Not to my knowledge."

"Could he have been in town and you not know about it?"

"Easily," she says. "Elvira did not confide in me."

I nod, moving the pieces around in my brain. "And after you found the suite empty, then what?"

"I went to my room on the sixth floor, shed my duds, slipped under the covers and went to sleep," she says.

"What? No pajamas?"

"No nothing," she smiles. She glances at her wrist watch. "Are we through here? I have an appointment."

"With who?" I ask brazenly.

"It's whom, and it's none of your business."

She stands and puts out her hand. "It's been a delightful afternoon, Joe. You're good company even if you are a little too nosy, but I want you to know, I haven't given up on you yet."

I smile taking her hand.

"Good to know," I say.

She winks at me and then strolls away, again swinging her body in a most lascivious manner. I try to picture her killing Bryce Tremayne and I can't. For the time being I cross her off my list.

CHAPTER TEN

I arrive home a little after six with a bagful of groceries on the seat next to me. I pull into the driveway and park. I can't use the garage because Bunny's Plymouth is housed there, awaiting her return. I think the car and I are both looking at a long wait.

As I exit my car I look across the street where a black Ford sedan is parked. It screams "Cop!" and sure enough, out from behind the wheel comes Shorty, the rude little guy who caught up with me at the YMCA gym. This time he is without his partner, no doubt under the impression that he can handle the likes of me without backup. We meet at my front stoop.

"The lieutenant wants to see you," Shorty says brusquely. "Let's go."

"Have him come to my office in the morning."

"Now."

"Can't now," I say. "I'm about to have supper."

I start toward my front door but Shorty blocks my way.

"Your supper can wait."

"Hey, would you mind? The ice cream's melting and the beer's getting warm."

He shakes his head.

"Now, wise guy."

He flips open his jacket so I can see his .38 police special nestled in a shoulder holster.

"Wow," I say in awe. "A gun. Are you planning to shoot me right here on my front lawn? Maybe we should sell tickets."

He shakes his head, muttering a barely audible "Jesus Christ". He looks at me. I look at him. Finally he gets the message. "Would you please accompany me to division headquarters, sir?"

I smile. "I'd be delighted to, as soon as I put away the groceries."

I drive myself with Shorty following, mainly because I don't want to be in the same car with the little twerp. I find Lt. Overton in an interrogation room perusing some paperwork. He has a mug of coffee and a manila envelope at his side and a half lit cigar in an ashtray. He smiles up at me as I enter and rises to shake my hand.

"Thank you for coming, Mr. Bernardi. I hope I haven't interrupted any supper plans."

"Not a problem, Lieutenant. I'm dining informally this evening."

"Good, good," he says. "I suppose you are aware that we have excluded Mr. Kazan as a suspect."

"I gathered as much."

"Yes, there was no indication that he had left the lot that night and besides, one of the security guards, checking offices, found him sleeping on his office sofa at around three o'clock. Anyway, we're looking elsewhere."

"Well, a man like Tremayne," I say, "I imagine you have no shortage of suspects."

"You're right about that, sir," Overton says. "Absolutely." He picks up the half a stogie and lights it with a kitchen match he takes from his shirt pocket. "Why, we have one man close to the case who was in an elevator and overheard a man say, 'Someone ought to kill the son of a bitch'." He smiles.

"That would be me," I say.

"Indeed it would," Overton says.

"Does that mean I'm back on your shit list?"

"I don't know, Mr. Bernardi. Should you be?"

He opens the middle drawer of the desk and rummages, looking for something. He doesn't find it so he tries the side drawers and then, in disgust, shakes his head sheepishly and picks up the manila envelope.

"Have you ever met Roscoe Heep, Mr. Bernardi?" he asks.

"Sure. House detective at the Biltmore."

He slides a glossy photo out of the envelope and pushes it toward me. "Did he ever show you this photograph?"

I look. It's the lobby picture of Annie Petrakis.

"Yes, he did."

"And did you deny knowing who this woman was?"

I smell a trap coming on.

"Sure. He wasn't the police. It was none of his business."

"But you do know her name."

"Ann Petrakis. She works makeup at the studio."

Overton seems to relax a littlle. "Ah, then you didn't know her well," he says with a smile.

"Hardly at all," I say.

He frowns. "Curious," he says. "Then why did we find your business card with your home telephone number on the back in her purse?"

Ooops. That one I didn't smell coming.

Overton starts smiling again. "Now here's the problem, Mr. Bernardi, I'd like to believe that you're just a bystander in all this but just when I'm about to arrive at that conclusion, something else pops up. Like your card. Now as you know from Mr. Heep, Miss Petrakis was making a pest of herself at the Biltmore, trying to get in to see Mr. Tremayne the afternoon of the day he was killed. And early this afternoon, metro officers aided by this photo, were able to detain her from taking a bus trip to Phoenix where, apparently, she knows no one. Do you know anything about that?"

"No, I don't."

"She had a large suitcase with her. All of her belongings. I don't think she was coming back."

He stares at me. I stare back.

"Well?" he says finally.

"Well what?" I ask.

"Answer my question."

"What question?"

"About Phoenix."

"You didn't ask me about Phoenix."

"Are you sure?"

"Positive."

He screws up his face and scratches his head.

"Why did you give her your card?" he asks.

"I'm sure she's already told you that."

"But I'd like to hear it from you."

He takes out a pencil, ready to take notes on the back of the manila envelope. I tell him about Ray Kravitz and the column full of lies and her eviction from her apartment and my offer to help if I can. He nods and puts down the pencil.

"That's about what she said. All right, Mr. Bernardi, you're free to go."

"Miss Petrakis. Would it possible to speak with her?"

"Not at this time," Overton says.

"Has she been charged?"

"Not yet."

"Does she have a lawyer?"

"None I'm aware of," Overton says.

I get to my feet and head for the door. "You don't mind if I get her one." I say.

He shrugs. "It's the beauty of America," he says. "Land of the free though I guess there's nothing free about lawyers."

"And I guess they're ever grateful to guys like you for keeping them in business. Come on, Lieutenant, you and I both know that Annie Petrakis didn't kill anyone," I say with more hope than certitude.

"Do we?" he says with a faint smile.

"We do and you'd probably admit it if you weren't trying so hard to distract me with that Harry Hayseed act of yours."

"Why, Mr. Bernardi, are you accusing me of dissembling?" he asks

"If you were as absentminded as you pretend to be, Lieutenant, you'd still be walking a beat in Bell Gardens."

"Driving a squad car."

"What?"

"Driving a squad car, Mr. Bernardi. Nobody walks in Los Angeles, not even the police."

"Drive, walk, I don't care, just as long as you get off your butt and find out who really killed Bryce Tremayne."

With that, I stomp out indignantly.

When I arrive home, I go straight to the phone and call Ray Giordano. I tell him all about Annie and the fact that she's being held at Van Nuys Station. No, I tell him testily, this is not another one of my freebies. I'll be responsible for the bill. I know he's having fun at my expense but when I tell him some of the grimier details of the case, the kidding stops and he gets serious. Suddenly I'm aware that he can't wait to get at it. A nationally known columnist is murdered in the shadow of a movie studio. Sexual overtones put it on page one and best of all, he has an attractive and vulnerable defendant. Cases like this made Darrow a celebrity overnight. Ray says he'll talk to Annie within the hour and give me a full report in the morning.

I hang up and go into the kitchen where I encounter disaster. In my haste to get my visit to the cops over with, I put the chopped chuck in the freezer and the ice cream in the refrigerator. Now I have a clump of hamburger I can use as a deadly weapon and a carton of goop that used to be cherry vanilla. Weary and disgusted I break out the Coors, haul a bag of chips from the top of the cabinet and settle down in front of the television set. Sunday night. Ed Sullivan. The picture comes onscreen. Oh, boy. Senor Wences. One of my favorites. For a moment I'm forced to think about the case as an image of Basil Rathbone as Sherlock Holmes pops into my brain. He's smiling at me, one eyebrow arched quizzically.

I think, easy for him, difficult for me.

CHAPTER ELEVEN

t's Monday morning. The first day of shooting. I'm at the studio by 7:30 and on the set by 8:00. In some quarters it's considered good luck to be on the premises when the camera rolls for the first take and I'm as superstitious as the next guy. When I walk in Kazan is setting up the scene where Blanche, played by Vivien Leigh, first enters the Kowalski apartment. Brando's in the scene. So is Kim Hunter.

Kazan's in deep conversation with Harry Stradling, the cinematographer, so I wander over to the craft services table and grab myself a cup of joe. Brando's there trying to decide between a peach danish and a cruller.

"Good morning, Mr. Brando," I say.

He looks up, curious for just a moment and then he smiles in recognition. "Morning, Joe. And none of that mister stuff. Call me Bud"

"Sure," I say. "Ready to go?"

"Always ready, man."

He chooses the cruller and takes a healthy bite. "Hey, this is good," he says, taking a second bite.

"Have you met Miss Leigh yet?" I ask.

"Miss Leigh? Oh, yeah, Miss Leigh. Yeah, she seems okay, I

guess. A little, uh--what am I trying to stay? Stand offish. Cold fish. Well, what the hell, she's British, right? They're all like that."

"Maybe not all, but I know what you mean," I say.

He shakes his head searching for something else to eat. "Don't know why they couldn't have hired Jessie. She woulda been terrific."

Jessie is Jessica Tandy who originated the role on Broadway. She's the only major cast member that didn't make the transition to the film and I sense Brando has a real issue with that.

"Well, I guess they felt she didn't have the name," I say.

He looks at me with a disbelieving scowl. "And I do? I do? Maybe they should have just hired Julie and this British babe and screwed the picture up entirely."

"Julie?" I say blankly,

"Garfield," he says. "They offered it to Julie first. I happen to know that for a fact. I was like second choice. Maybe not even that. Me, I'm gonna be okay, but this Miss Leigh, I don't know. I just don't know. I think they shoulda gjven Jessie some consideration."

By now he's found a second cruller and he wanders off, shaking his head and talking to himself. I wonder how many other cast members share his opinion and whether it will hurt the picture. Probably not but the chances for a happy set seem to be dimming.

"Good morning, Joe."

I turn to the voice at my elbow. It's Kazan.

"Good morning, Mr.---Gadge," I say, catching myself.

"I want to thank you. Great job getting the police out of my hair."

"It's what they pay me for. In your case, it was a pleasure."

"Well, thanks again," he says.

"Sure. What about the hearings?"

He shrugs. "My agent says he talked to Warner who says they're going to let me finish the picture and by that time, the committee may have suspended the hearings, at least for the remainder of the year."

"So you dodged a bullet," I say.

"Temporary, Joe. Just temporary. Fascist bastards like Wood and the others never quit. God won't let them." He picks up an apple and takes a bite. "By the way, I talked to Tom last night. He sends regards." Tom is Tennessee Williams who wrote the screenplay based on his script. We got to know each other while the studio was filming 'The Glass Menagerie'.

"How is he?" I ask.

"Well. He and Frank have taken a place in Nice for the summer." Frank Merlo is Williams' longtime companion. "That's one of the perquisites of being a writer, Joe. You work when you want and where you want and not a soul can say you nay."

He smiles and I smile back. Directors may be the big cheeses on a production but their hours are brutal and sleep is a luxury.

"I'm sorry I'm not going to see him. I half thought he might be here for the shoot."

Kazan laughs. "Hardly. When he departed he left his script in my hands with a heavy heart."

"How so?" I ask.

"He's a torn man, Joe. On one hand he's happy and proud that his work is being filmed. On the other hand, he is sick over the compromises and changes that were forced on him."

I nod. "Yes. I can imagine."

"Anyway, I will fight as best I can to maintain the integrity of his work but I know already it is not going to be easy."

"The Catholic Decency League?"

He shrugs philosophically. "And that's just for starters." He looks over toward the set. "Excuse me, I think I'd better go rehearse my actors. Thanks again for all your help."

I watch as he makes his way onto the set where the cast members are waiting. Brando is kidding around with Kim Hunter who apparently gives as good as she gets. Vivien Leigh is standing off to one side, isolated, checking her makeup with a compact mirror. Odd woman out, I think.

I head back to the office. Glenda Mae has arrived. My mail has been sorted and only those that look special have been placed on my desk next to the morning Times and the trade papers. She brings me coffee and tells me I have had several calls including one from Ray Giordano. I ask her to get him on the phone. I sit back, sip the coffee and pick up a postcard depicting the French Riviera. The message is short. "Hope you are enjoying the depressing, stultifying and nauseating atmosphere of the studio. As you can see, I am not. Love, Tom. P.S. Frank sends regards". I'm reminded of another postcard I received from him many months back from the Bahamas. "Have just finished reading your novel. Brilliant. America's reading public apparently not so brilliant. Condolences." Williams has the life. I wish I had it. Maybe some day.

Glenda Mae buzzes the intercom and I pick up the phone.

"Let me guess," I say. "You've sprung her on her own recognizance."

"Hardly," Ray says. "I have a ten o'clock with an assistant D.A. to see if we can work something out."

"Has she been charged?"

"Not yet."

"What do you think?" I ask.

"I think your lady friend could be in a heap of trouble."

"Let me guess. She had dinner with Tremayne at Chasen's on Friday night, hours before he was killed."

"Wrong," Ray says. "But she was there."

"Tell me."

"After she got booted from the Biltmore lobby on Friday afternoon, she waited across the street, still hoping to get a chance to confront Tremayne. She had a long wait. Around seven thirty, Tremayne comes out and grabs a cab."

"Alone?"

"Alone. Annie hails another cab and follows him to Chasens restaurant. She's about to go in when through one of those front windows that face Beverly Boulevard she sees him sit down at a table where a man is already seated."

"Man. Not a woman."

"Man. His back is to her so she can't see who it is or what he looks like so she does what she's been doing all afternoon. She picks a spot and waits. After about a half hour the guy gets up, maybe to go to the john, who knows? She's too far away to get a good look at him. While he's away from the table this young woman comes into the restaurant and goes straight to Tremayne."

"His secretary, Jenny Coughlin."

"Really?"

"Really. Continue," I say.

"Anyway, Tremayne starts yammering at her and she heads out of there under an obvious head of steam. A minute or so later Tremayne's dinner companion reappears and takes his seat. They talk, they drink coffee and after about thirty minutes they get up to leave. In a moment, they appear at the front entrance. The companion lingers in the doorway and waves goodbye to Tremayne as he gets into a cab. The cab takes off and right away a car parked at curbside takes off in pursuit."

"The bodyguards. Did she say what kind of car it was?"

"I asked her," Ray says. "She doesn't know from cars."

"What about the companion in the doorway? Did she get a decent look at him?"

"Sort of. Enough to know he has white hair and a white mustache and is maybe 60 or so. Other than that, average height, average build, average everything."

"And Tremayne. Did Annie follow him again?"

"She couldn't. No cabs around. She says at that point she gave up and went back to the house where she was staying, let herself in and went to bed."

"Let herself in? You mean, there was no one home?"

"No, the people she was staying with had gone away for the weekend."

"Damn," I mutter quietly.

"You said it, Joe. No alibi for the time of death."

"Okay, so what's next?"

"Like I said, I play nice with the D.A. If he's a good guy he lets her go while they sort things out. If not, they've got another day they can hold her and then they either charge her or kick her loose."

"Be nice if we could find out who that guy was at Chasens before the cops do," I say.

"Cops don't know about him. Annie was smart enough to keep her mouth shut until I got to her. I told her to keep it up. If they have questions, refer them to me."

"What about Chasens?" I ask.

"No can do, Joe. Not today. I've got a full load," Ray says.

"And I don't? Never mind. I gotta eat lunch somewhere. Leave it to me."

I hang up, intrigued by the identity of this mystery man. Yes,

I suppose it could be some old queen that Tremayne picked up at the Naked Apollo, but I can't see him exposing himself to that sort of scrutiny. No, whoever the man was, he fits in some other way.

As for Annie Petrakis, things could be better but they could also be a lot worse. I can't worry about it because at the moment I am building up a full workload of my own. The phone has been ringing constantly while I was talking to Ray and I don't have to be Einstein to figure out what's happening. The sharks are circling, everyone from Hedda to Louella to Sheila Graham and Jimmie Fidler, the wire services and the major dailies. What happened to the Tremayne column about Kazan? Did Jack Warner have it squelched? How come Kazan's not a suspect? Why hasn't shooting on 'Streetcar' been postponed? And so on and so on. I sigh audibly. It's going to be a hard, hard day.

By noon my left ear hurts and my right hand has writer's cramp. I suspect that tomorrow's press coverage will be ugly. No matter what I had to say, nobody was happy with my answers. Ever since 1924 when producer Thomas Ince died aboard William Randolph Hearst's luxury yacht, perhaps shot by Hearst himself, the press has been tenacious when it comes to celebrity murders. Was Hearst arrested? No, he wasn't even questioned and after months of lies, distractions, outraged denials and clumsy coverups, the incident was consigned to the dustbin marked 'Who cares any more?" and was forgotten by all but the conspiracy zealots. Yes, tomorrow's coverage is going to be very interesting and possibly very ugly. Meanwhile it is now clear that Annie Petrakis hasn't a prayer of keeping her name out of this and as much as I would like to wash my hands of the whole sordid business, I know I can't. Me and my big mouth. I'm the guy who said, 'Somebody ought to kill the son of a bitch.'

Which reminds me...

I call the Biltmore and ask for John Smith. I'm surprised when my quarry answers the phone himself.

"Mr. Cox, it's Joe Bernardi from Warner Brothers."

"Oh, hello," he says without enthusiasm.

"I thought if you weren't busy you might let me buy you lunch," I say.

"What? Oh, well, I'm very sorry but---"

"I thought I'd fill you in on the truth about where your boss died and how and what the police know that they aren't talking about."

There is a moment's silence and then he says, "Well, then, yes, of course. I'd be delighted."

"Good," I say. "Chasen's. One o'clock. The reservation's under my name."

I hang up and ask Glenda Mae to make the reservation and then to get me Lieutenant Overton. It takes ten minutes but he finally comes in the line.

"Mr. Bernardi, I really very busy just now---"

"Just one question, Lieutenant, and I'll let you go. The matchbook from the Naked Apollo, was it new or used and secondly, did you find any fingerprints?"

"It was used and there was one set of prints, unidentified."

"Thanks."

"Could you tell me---?"

Too late. I've hung up. The phone rings. I ignore it and head out for Chasens where outside, the valet takes my car and inside, Raoul, the maitre'd takes me to a nice table over near a window. Cox arrives a few minutes behind me. He's wearing a baby blue sport jacket, a pale yellow collared shirt and a navy ascot. When he sits I catch a whiff of gardenias. I order a Coors. Cox opts for a mimosa. We exchange pleasantries. I ask about his plans. He has none. Hearst has extended the suite through the coming weekend as a courtesy to the police who want everyone to be available if needed over the next few days. The column is as dead as Tremayne until Hearst can dig up a new and improved firebrand hate monger. Cox seems to be taking it all calmly. If he's worried about his future he doesn't show it.

"And so, Mr. Bernardi, I was intrigued by your phone call."

I nod. "Just as I was intrigued the other day at your suggestion that there were things to be found by digging into Bryce Tremayne's past."

"All of which is now moot," he says.

"Maybe not," I say. "We still have an unidentified killer running around loose. I would say that everything about Bryce Tremayne, past and present, is fair game."

"Yes, perhaps you're right," Cox says. He takes a half-empty pack of Camels from his shirt pocket and reaches over for a matchbook that's tucked in a holder affixed to the ashtray. He lights up and sticks the matchbook in his shirt pocket.

"So, Mr. Cox," I say, "you've been here in town for over a week."

"More like ten days," he says.

"And have you discovered the joys of the Naked Apollo?"

He gives me a slit-eyed stare. "I thought we were here to discuss Bryce Tremayne," he says.

"Everything's on the table, Mr. Cox. What was so damning about Tremayne's past that you felt I needed to know about it."

Cox hesitates, a sure sign that a prevarication is on its way. "He was a tough judge of people's failings. He made a lot of enemies."

The waiter brings our drinks. I hold my tongue until he's gone.

"The police found a matchbook from the Naked Apollo in his shirt pocket. Want to revise that answer?"

I catch him by surprise and he glares at me.

"I wouldn't know---"

"Of course you know. Tell me or tell the police. Up to you. And by the way, even a blind umpire can see which side of the plate you're swinging from. I don't care. You are not the issue. Bryce Tremayne is."

"You want me to tell you that Bryce was homosexual."

"Only if it's true."

"It's not true. Not really. The fact was, Bryce was not fussy. Some people like their eggs over easy. Bryce was into soft boiled, hard boiled, omelets, scrambled, shirred and poached.

I smile, trying hard to suppress a laugh. "And yea, even unto the animals in the meadow."

Now Cox smiles. "I doubt even Bryce went that far."

The waiter comes by and since we're both hungry, we order, along with a couple of fresh drinks. I watch him walk away before I turn back to Cox.

"So after he destroys you in several of his columns, you two become close friends," I say.

Cox shakes his head. "Even before the columns," he says.

Now it's my turn to be surprised. "Nice guy," I say.

"Never, but he could separate his job from his personal life."

"And you had no other place to go."

"No, I didn't." He polishes off the remains of his first drink in one swallow.

I smile. "Well, Mr. Cox. for an indentured servant you don't have it so bad. Expensive suits, an eye-popping emerald pinkie ring, living in suites in the best hotels---"

He interrupts me. "It's bad enough I have to work with those people. I don't have to live with them. A friend has lent me the use of his Malibu beach house for the duration of my stay."

"Nice friend."

"He's sunning himself in St.Tropez for the next few weeks accompanied by another good friend of his. An even better friend than me."

"Gotcha," I say with a smile. "Now, about the Naked Apollo."

"I've dropped by there several times," he says.

"By yourself?"

"You mean without Bryce?" He shakes his head. "I went by myself."

"Do you know if Bryce went there without you?"

"He didn't. He would never take the chance. His enemies would destroy him if it ever got out." He furrows his brow. "Tell me, Mr. Bernardi, why this preoccupation with Bryce's sex life?"

I tell him how the body was found. He stares at me in disbelief.

"My God," he says.

"Yes, my God," I repeat.

At this moment Dave Chasen approaches the table. I'm well enough known that I rate a greeting from the man himself.

"Joe, so nice to see you," he says.

"You, too, Dave." I introduce Cox. The two men shake.

He looks at me, shaking his head. "Bad business, all that stuff with Kazan. You must be up to your knees in it."

"Higher," I say with a grin.

"Anything I can do for you?" he asks.

"Actually, yes. Bryce Tremayne had dinner here Friday night."

"Yes, I heard."

"He had a dinner guest."

"Heard that, too."

"Do you remember his name?" I ask.

"Sorry, Joe. Never met him. I wasn't here Friday."

"Is there someone here who might have caught his name or at least be able to describe him?"

"Important?"

"Very."

"Let me check," Dave says as he walks off.

Cox eyes me suspiciously. "Playing detective?"

"Not really," I say. "Just curious."

In a moment Dave returns accompanied by a very pretty and petite cocktail waitress.

"This is Alicia. She served them drinks Friday evening."

I smile and introduce myself. Yes, she remembers Mr. Tremayne's guest but she never heard his name and she is also pretty sure he's never been in the restaurant before.

"Could you describe him?" I ask.

"Sure," she says. "Older gentleman. Suntanned, a nice full head of white hair, a white mustache.'

I sense a movement out of the corner of my eye. Cox has twitched and as I look at his face, I know he's onto something.

"But no name."

"No."

"What about their waiter?" I ask.

"I checked Friday's schedule. Luis had their table."

"Is he around?"

Dave shakes his head. "He left the next morning for Mexico City. His mother is very ill. I have no idea when he'll be back."

I nod and thank Dave for his help and as I watch him and Alice walk away, I turn to Cox.

"Anything you want to say?"

"Like what?"

"You seemed to recognize that description."

He laughs. "Description? That could have been a hundred guys including Santa Claus."

Lunch comes and we eat. As we get ready to leave I make another stab at the identity of Tremayne's guest but Cox's story stays the same. He has no idea who it could have been. He's a liar and liars will be outed but I just hope it comes soon.

CHAPTER TWELVE

It's a lousy afternoon. Really lousy. I need to be sharp and I'm not. Three beers at Chasen's took care of that. The wires and the phone calls keep piling up. For the most part they're the Kazan haters, the ones who desperately need to savage the director to bolster their own preconceived notions. There is no way to deal with them except to deny, deny and deny. It's all I can do to keep my temper in check. There are some butterflies among the hornets, people like Phineas Ogilvy and Lacey Hightower who replaced Bunny at The Hollywood Reporter. I give them lots of time and attention and I know they will reciprocate by printing the facts and nothing but the facts. Hedda Hopper has called twice and twice Glenda Mae has been able to put her off. Now the phone rings again and when Glenda Mae buzzes me, she's furious.

"Pardon my french, boss," she says, "but that no talent bitch is on the line cussin' me out."

"Hedda?"

"Who else?"

"I'll take it." I punch the lit phone button and fake enthusiasm. "Hedda, I can't believe I missed you twice. How are you, love?"

"Save that canned bullshit for the Des Moines Register, Bernardi. I know when I'm being jerked around."

"Absolutely untrue. I just got back to the office after a long and lousy lunch."

"The rest of your afternoon is going to be even lousier if you don't give me some straight answers. Who paid off the cops to clear Kazan? Warner?"

"Nobody paid anything to anybody," I say.

"Tell that to Louella but not to me, sweetie. I read the piece in the Sunday Times by that pansy Ogilvy. Is he on your payroll?"

"Careful, Hedda, there are laws."

"Screw the laws. Tremayne threatens to expose Kazan in a big Sunday column. Tremayne gets killed and the column never appears. Even us journalists can put that together."

I am starting to seethe. This is the woman who revealed the Tracy-Hepburn relationship, accused Joe Cotten of having an affair with Deanna Durbin and did her damnedest to paint Cary Grant and Randolph Scott as homosexual lovers. She has claws like razors and she loves to use them.

"Oh, so now you're a journalist, Hedda. When did that happen?"

"Don't get smart with me, honey. I can have your job."

"And welcome to it. Look, Hedda, there's no hanky-panky, no secret deals. I messengered over a press release with all the facts and nothing but the facts. That's the story. There is nothing else."

"You say."

I pause for a moment to bait the hook.

"I thought you were anxious to get a face to face with Marlon Brando," I say.

"You know perfectly well I can't get through to him. Nobody can," she says.

"I can," I say.

The silence from Hedda's end is deafening.

"Meaning?"

"Meaning you haven't got a prayer in hell of ever getting to him as long as you're going to trash Kazan. They are very very close."

"But?"

"You might want to write a paragraph or two complimenting the police on their diligence in clearing Mr. Kazan of any involvement, perhaps describing their investigation as an excellent example of American justice at work. Make it about the police and not Kazan and keep your claws sheathed."

"And?"

"And I will talk to Brando and put in a good word for you. No guarantees."

"Oh, no, that's not----"

"I'm looking forward to reading your column tomorrow, Hedda. And now you'll have to excuse me, I'm very busy taking phone calls from idiots." I hang up and tell Glenda Mae not to put her through if she calls back.

I had swiveled my desk chair around so that I was looking out the window at the activity in the street below. Now I swivel back to my desk and look up in surprise to see Lt. Lloyd Overton standing in my open doorway, leaning against the door jamb with a smile in his face.

"Good for you. I don't like that woman. Never have."

"I will admit, she brings out the worst in me," I say.

He steps into the room, leaning on his cane.

"May I?" he asks.

I gesture toward my visitor's chair and he sits. I offer him something to drink but he just shakes his head.

"I find you interesting, Mr. Bernardi," he says.

"Thank you."

"I'm not sure that's a compliment. You're something of an oddball in our circles, sticking your nose into police business, playing amateur detective, emphasis on the amateur."

"It's nothing I do willingly, Lieutenant, believe me," I say.

He just smiles. "Nevertheless." He pats at his jacket , then at his shirt pocket and then takes out a half smoked cigar. "Do you have something I can use as an ashtray?" he asks.

I reach into a desk drawer and produce one. I keep it for guests. He smiles. "Very nice. Thank you," he says. He fumbles a bit more, looking through his pockets. I reach in the drawer again, find a book of matches and slide it across the desk. He nods and smiles again as he lights up. If that cigar cost more than a dime I'd be surprised.

"Why were you having lunch with Hubbell Cox?" he asks when the initial cloud of smoke clears.

"Now you're having me followed."

"No, we're following Hubbell Cox."

"The matchbook," I say.

"Yes, we found his prints on it."

"An obvious plant," I say.

"Yes, even we professionials were able to figure that one out."

"And do you figure that Cox planted it?"

"I don't know. He seems bright enough, too bright to leave his fingerprints for us to find."

"A frame?" I ask.

"Either that or someone wanted Mr. Tremayne's murder to look like a homosexual killing and just got careless. What did you and Mr. Cox talk about?"

I shrug. "Texas, horses, the weather, and the love that dares not speak its name."

He looks at me, almost amused, but there's flint in his eyes.

"Look, Mr. Bernardi, I understand your involvement with the Petrakis woman. She came to you. You tried to help. But now I'm starting to think you're playing detective again and that won't do. Not for a moment. Now I ask you again, what did you talk about?"

I stare at him for several moments and then I buzz Glenda Mae. When she comes on line I ask her to get me the gentleman whose name begins with K, the one she's so happy to see whenever he drops into the office unannounced. Within a minute she double buzzes me and I pick up the phone.

"I'm sitting here with homicide lieutenant Lloyd Overton. What do you think of him?" I listen. "Can I trust him?" I listen some more. "Throw him how far?" More listening. "Okay, thanks. If this backfires on me, I'm coming after your first born."

I hang up.

"Apparently you can be trusted." I tell him about Cox's cryptic remark in the elevator and the revelation over lunch about Tremayne's eclectic taste in sex partners. I can tell I've given him something he didn't have.

He nods. "And that's it?"

"That's it," I say.

"Excellent, Mr. Bernardi. Thank you."

He and his cigar get up and head for the door. He turns back toward me. "Will you please tell Sergeant Kleinschmidt that I appreciate his ringing endorsement. I will do the same for him some time." And he walks out.

I spend the rest of the afternoon fending off the jackals. Some woman from Women's Wear Daily calls to laud the police for their integrity in absolving Kazan of any involvement while on the other hand I get the feeling she wants to extol Kazan for getting rid of Tremayne once and for all. I make a mental note to read this one. It ought to be a dilly.

I finally get to leave around six-thirty. The company has wrapped for the day. Things went smoothly. Tempers did not flare. Tantrums were not in evidence. I pull into my driveway near seven. I never noticed the strange car across the street which is why I am startled when two men step out of the bushes a few yards away from my kitchen door.

Willie Babbitt looks even less friendly than the last time I saw him. As he moves toward me Little Bob Brown follows in his wake, poker faced and silent as usual.

"Hold up there, fella," Willie says.

I don't like the looks of this situation so I give him my hard look.

"You're trespassing. Get off my property."

"I have a message for you, smart ass. Mind your own business," he says.

"Thanks for coming. Now get lost."

Willie takes two more steps toward me, his right hand a fist and his left rubbing it, getting ready for action. He smiles. Not friendly. One of anticipation.

"I don't want to hurt you-----"

"But. Listen, gargantua, I've already described you and the munchkin here to the police. Phineas Ogilvy is ready to press charges over the other day and if you lay a hand on me, I'll see they put you away for at least a year."

Our voices have gotten louder. Or at least mine has. Willie is still speaking in a low venomous whisper.

"If I lay a hand on you, you won't be in a position to talk to anybody for a long time," Willie says.

"Get the hell off my property, you son of a bitch!" I scream at him.

He responds even more quietly. "I repeat, stop sticking your nose where it don't belong or next time I see you, I will kill you."

At this point my neighbor Chuck Bledsoe appears around the corner of his house. Chuck is six-two and a former UCLA linebacker. He's also a good neighbor. I borrow his hedge trimmer and return it right away. He borrows my lawnmower and I don't see it for a month. When I go to get it, he apologizes and asks if he can borrow my wheelbarrow. He's that kind of a neighbor and he is a good guy.

"I heard voices," he says. "What's going on?"

"Chuck, go back inside and call the police."

He frowns, puzzled, and takes a step forward.

"Now, Chuck! " I tell him. "They're carrying guns."

Chuck gets the message and hurries back to his front door.

Willie steps toward me again. We're inches apart. His halitosis is overwhelming me.

"Next time the neighbor ain't gonna be around to save your ass, snoopy boy. Remember what I said. This is none of your business. Wise up." With that he turns, head nods to Little Bob Brown, and the two of them hot foot it across the street to their car.

I watch them go and then hurry to Chuck's front door to tell him to call off the police. Boris and Bela have left the premises.

I treat myself to a lousy dinner of franks and beans, eat half of it and throw the rest into the garbage pail. My stomach's in a knot. I have no wish to have the crap beaten out of me by the likes of Willie Babbitt nor do I wish to let Willie Babbitt dictate how I am going to lead my life. For that reason alone I am not going to back off.

I uncap a beer from the six pack in the fridge and go into

the living room. I plop down in front of the TV set but I don't turn it on. I take a deep swig as thoughts swirl around my brain and I remember the look on Hubbell Cox's face when I described Tremayne's dinner companion the night he was killed. That was lunch and six hours later I'm being belly-bumped by a Neanderthal in a cheap suit. Coincidence? I think not but what it means I have no idea.

I realize my bottle is empty. I go into the kitchen and get another and as I return to my perch, I think of Father Brian, the alcoholic priest who runs the Alcoholics Anonymous meeting over at St. Stephen's church in Boyle Heights. I realize now that I am stopping every evening on the way home for groceries and that every evening I am also picking up a six pack of Coors. How long before I start showing up at the church basement and begin raising my hand? I don't need Father Brian to tell me what my problem is. She's three thousand miles away, awhirl in a social environment I have no real use for and I am desperately afraid it is changing her and not for the better. I take a long draught of the beer. It helps but not a lot. I'm wallowing in self pity and though I don't like It, I don't know what to do about it. Beg her to come back to me? Quit my job and move to New York? Come to grips with the thought that we are two different people with different life agendas that no amount of love can overcome? I mull that last one for only a moment. It's much too real to seriously contemplate. For the time being I'll continue to let the beer cast a blanket of denial over my feelings or as Scarlet O'Hara so famously said, "I'll think about it tomorrow."

CHAPTER THIRTEEN

bout Hedda---" Charlie was saying.

I raise my hands defensively.

"I'm sorry. I couldn't help it but the bitch asked for it. Am I fired?"

"What are you talking about?" Charlie says. He points to the morning Times. "If you're responsible for this, I may give you a raise."

I pick up the paper, scan Hedda's column and smile. It was everything I could have hoped for. The Los Angeles police are stalwart guardians of people's rights. Justice is blind. We should all be grateful that we live in a country where every man is protected from government badgering and reprisals regardless of political beliefs. 'Elia Kazan has been cleared of any involvement in the death of Bryce Tremayne and that's good enough for me', she writes.

I put the paper back on Charlie's desk with a smile.

"Now all I have to do is deliver Brando for an interview with her highness," I say.

Charlie laughs out loud.

"Good luck, knucklehead," he says.

I'm incensed. "You think I can't do it?"

"Not likely," he says.

I smile. "For five bucks?"

"You're on."

We shake.

"So what was it the bitch asked for?" Charlie asks.

I tell him about our conversation and he laughs again.

"I'll tell Jack. He'll get a kick out of it."

I nod. "You know there was a time when we were afraid of those people."

"I remember," Charlie says. "Maybe it was the war that changed all that. Hedda's losing outlets. Louella's readership is down. Hearst is lying in his bed in Beverly Hills dying. I hear he hasn't got much longer. It's a different world now, Joe."

"You mean I have permission to blow these people off if they get too pushy?"

"Absolutely," he says and then adds, "but check with me first."

He laughs again and I realize it's the first time in months that Charlie has actually laughed out loud. Maybe the twins ran away from home.

I go to my office which I haven't been to yet since Charlie waylaid me in the parking lot and hustled me up to his office. Glenda Mae's her usual ebullient self. I have no calls and not much mail. I say yes to coffee and go into my private sanctum. I decide I have to go to the set and talk to Brando. I give it a moment's thought and decide I'll put it off until later. Much later.

Glenda Mae brings coffee and I ask her to get me Lt. Overton. When he comes on the line, I tell him about my encounter the previous evening outside my kitchen door.

"One guy is a named Willie Babbitt---"I say.

"And the other is Little Bob Brown," he continues it for me.

"We checked San Antonio police as soon as we found out they had worked for Tremayne. You've run afoul of a couple of really bad dudes, Mr. Bernardi. Rap sheets that go back before the war. Both have done stretches in a Texas state prison. At the moment they are clean. No warrants out but I'd steer clear of them."

"I would if I could, Lieutenant, but they keep forcing their attention on me."

"You want me to pick them up?"

"On what charge? Abuse of the English language? Last week they leaned on Phineas Ogilvy, the entertainment editor of the Times, but he's already told me he won't press charges."

"Be safer for you if I roust them a little," Overton says.

"But less educational," I say.

"You think they're involved?"

"Right now, I think everybody's involved. I just called to tell you that if anything happens to me, they're the first two you should look at."

"I will," Overton says, "and if you're still alive, I'll report whatever they have to say."

I chuckle. "Lieutenant, you just cracked a joke."

"We officers of the law are not without a sense of humor, Mr. Bernardi," he says.

If so, it's the first I've heard of it but I let it pass and a moment later I hang up. I have accomplished my purpose by putting Overton on notice. I'm a private citizen scared of a couple of known violent criminals. I therefore am within my rights to defend myself and so I now feel a lot better about the Beretta.25 automatic that I carry in my jacket pocket. I have had the gun for years and I also have a carry permit issued to me two years ago by the Los Angles County Sheriff's department. The comforting thing is, I know how to use it.

My next move is pretty obvious but I need to figure the best way to approach it. Nothing has changed my opinion since last evening. Cause and effect. I describe a mysterious dinner guest. Cox silently throws off a passel of "oh, shit" vibes and six hours later I get a visit from Laurel and Hardy's evil twins. I have to confront Cox and for a moment I consider a phone call. I have too much work to do on 'Streetcar' to be running all over L.A. On the other hand, a phone call gives him a chance to weasel and maybe even run for it. Like it or not, I'm headed for the Biltmore.

Halfway over the hill leading to the L.A. basin, traffic stops. I smell an accident ahead and my suspicions are confirmed when a squad car comes wailing by on the shoulder to my right. I settle in and flip on the radio, I'm immediately jarred by Debbie Reynolds and Carleton Carpenter jabbering 'Aba Daba Honeymoon'. I'm in no mood so I flip around and find a news station. World events are only slightly less depressing. Truman has just fired Doug MacArthur as commander in Korea and things are minimally better. Seoul is in sight but I really don't care. I just want the damned thing over with. They've just tested an atomic bomb at a site in Nevada. Great. Can mutual destruction be far behind? The last item is of no great interest except maybe to those of us in the business. They've just broadcast the first television signals in color from the tower atop the Empire State Building. How long before Jack and Zukor and Harry Cohn pull their heads out of the sand? You can't fight them forever. Maybe the time has come to join the parade.

The news broadcast ends to make way for Jimmie Fidler, the syndicated radio gossip columnist with nearly 500 outlets across the country. At this moment in time he probably has more clout than the rest of his peers combined. I'm immediately on guard. He's the only one I didn't hear from.

He doesn't waste any time. There's a massive coverup in play to protect Hollywood director Elia Kazan who was about to be exposed by the patriotic and newly martyred journalist Bryce Tremayne. How deeply was Kazan connected to the Tremayne murder and why is Warners throwing up a protective shield around their golden boy? And why are the cops mum on the details surrounding the death? The silence is oppressive as the Hollywood power brokers and the police conspire to keep their investigation under wraps. Maybe its time for another investigation, an investigation of the police and their cozy relationship with the ham-fisted moguls of Tinseltown.

The traffic starts to move and I have had enough of the Fidler so I go back to the previous station where Les Paul and Mary Ford are asking the musical question, 'How High The Moon'. An improvement. A big improvement.

Thirty minutes later I am pushing the button for the door chime of Suite 8001. At first there is no answer. I try again. Finally the door opens to reveal Elvira Tremayne clad in a nightgown and a silk bathrobe. She stares at me blankly and I try to figure if she's just gotten up or if she's gotten into the scotch.

"Joe Bernardi, Warner Brothers, Mrs. Tremayne," I say. "We met the other day." Technically we hadn't but there's no way she'll remember.

"Oh, yes," she smiles and then just stands there.

After a few moments, I say, "May I come in?"

"Oh, yes, certainly," she says, stepping aside. I walk in and look around as she shuts the door. "May I help you, Mr. Bernard?"

I overlook the mispronunciation. Now I'm pretty sure it's the scotch. I'm aided in this guess by the half-filled open bottle on the bar.

"I'm actually looking for Mr. Cox," I say.

"He stepped out early this morning," she says.

"Do you know where he went?"

"Not for certain but I can guess."

"Can you give me a hint?"

"I'd rather not."

"Are its initials Naked Apollo?"

She smiles and nods approvingly, then wanders toward the bar. "May I offer you a drink, Mr. Bernard?" she asks.

"Not just now. Any idea when he'll be back?"

"Don't know. Don't care."

There's an empty glass next to the bottle. She pours out four fingers and takes a swig. Just then the phone rings. Elvira walks behind the bar and answers it.

"Just got up," she says. "No ,no, I'm fine. Just tired.....I'm not dressed yet. Give me at least an hour......One o'clock. Okay.I'll be ready.....Jesus Christ! I said I'd be ready. Just leave me alone!" She slams the phone down.

I have pretended I wasn't listening but of course, I took in every word.

"Lunch date?"

"Is there something else I can do for you, Mr. Bernard?" she asks.

"How about Miss Coughlin? Is she around?" I ask.

"Certainly not," she replies huffily. "Miss Coughlin is no longer in our employ."

"Quit?"

"Fired. I have no need of the services she was providing my husband."

"Shorthand?"

She smiles patronizingly. "Is that supposed to pass for wit?"

"Only if your standards are low. Can you tell me how I can get in touch with Miss Coughlin?"

"I cannot," she says, "and would not if I were able. The little minx is out of my life. Let her stay there."

"A lot of things are out of your life, Mrs. Tremayne. My condolences."

She bursts into laughter. "Condolences! Ha. Very funny, sir. Thank you for your kind thoughts." She takes another healthy swig of the booze.

"Well, I'll get out of your way. I'm sure you have things to do."

We start toward the door.

"I have only one thing to do, Mr. Bernard. I must decide where to scatter my husband's ashes. I am torn between a landfill and the nearest drainage ditch."

She smiles as she opens the door and raises her glass to me. "Y'all take care now", she says with a suddenly discovered Texas drawl you could cut with a butter knife.

I smile and leave.

I'm beginning to feel very antsy about Hubbell Cox. There's something about him that I have distrusted since the first time I saw him. As much as I would rather not, I think I should stop by the Naked Apollo and, if necessary, drag him out of there at gunpoint. I have no beef with homosexuals. Our industry is crowded with them and one on one, ninety nine percent of them are delightful to be around. But in a group structure something happens that makes me very uncomfortable. Don't ask to explain it. I can't. Nonetheless, I have to confront Cox about the goons that waylaid me last evening and nothing is going to get in my way.

I get the address from the hotel concierge, who gives me a

funny look, and I drive over there. It's a tiny little place on a side street and when I arrive there are few cars around. I go in. It's dimly lit. There's a long mahogany bar along one wall and a single bartender lazily drying glasses with a towel. At the far end is a single patron, a strapping fellow who appears to be nursing a beer. Off in a corner I see two men sitting across from one another, hovering over a backgammon board. Otherwise the place is deserted.

I go to the bar and pull up a stool. The bartender gives me a long look, sizing me up. Finally he walks over to me. The stitching on his shirt says his name is Bruce. He's tall and beefy and though I'm sure that somewhere under the counter he has a baseball bat, I'm also sure that most of the time he doesn't need it

"What'll it be?" he asks.

"Coors on tap?" I ask.

He nods and reaches for a glass. He brings it over and sets it on a coaster. A perfect pour. Just the right amount of head. I take a deep swallow. It feels good going down.

"Mind if I ask you a question?" I say.

He smiles. "You can ask," he says, "as soon as you show me your badge."

"I'm not a cop," I say.

"Really?" He seems amused.

"Really," I say.

He shrugs. "Well, if you're not a cop, I think you're in the wrong place."

"I know where I am," I say. I lay my business card on the bar. The bartender looks at it. "I'm looking for a guy. I'd like to find him before the police do. That way everybody stays healthy and happy."

The bartender shakes his head. "I don't know him," he says.

"I haven't described him."

"I still don't know him. A couple of years ago a guy like you walked in here looking for someone. I helped him out. That night they found the guy outside his apartment house, half dead, badly beaten."

"It's not like that," I say.

"Sure," the bartender says with a smile as he walks off.

I hesitate for a moment, then walk down to the end of the bar and sit down next to the solitary drinker. He's a god looking guy with a twinkle in his eye and he looks over at me with a wry smile on his face.

"Not interested," he says,

"Me, either," I reply.

"My mistake," he says.

"Not a problem," I say, putting out my hand. "Joe Bernardi."

The big man shakes my hand. "Roy Fitzgerald."

"I'm in kind of a bind, Roy. The cops and I are both looking for the same guy and it'll be better for him if I find him first. I know he's been in here several times over the past week and a half."

"Good friend?" Roy asks and I know what he means.

"Just a friend but very concerned."

He narrows his eyes and looks me over carefully. "My second mistake," he says. "No offense."

"None taken."

"What's your friend's name?" Roy asks.

I tell him and then launch into a detailed description. Roy takes it all in, concentrating. When I'm finished he looks at me curiously. "Big emerald pinkie ring on his right hand?"

"That's him," I say.

"Yeah, he's been by a couple of times in the last week. Usually after nine o'clock. Stays until midnight. Drinks a lot but he can hold it."

"Does he hook up with anyone special?"

"Nope. He's a loner. Chats a lot. Once of twice he's gone up to the bandstand and sung with the combo but as far as cruising goes, he wasn't interested. He comes for the booze and the company of people he feels comfortable with."

"So there's nobody special?"

Roy grins. "Oh, there's somebody special, all right, but not around here."

"You're sure about that?"

Roy nods. "The signs are all there."

I take out my business card and slide it toward him.

"Thanks, Roy. You've been a big help. If he should come in, call me. Any time, day or night, home or office."

He picks up my card and scans it. He smiles at me. "Warner Brothers. Maybe one of these days we can do some business."

"Writer?"

"Actor. Universal's signing me up for their talent development program but if it doesn't pan out, maybe I'll come see you."

"I look forward to it," I say with a smile. I turn and walk out of the place.

I'm headed for my car when I look across the street. The car is painted Police Black and Shorty, the dwarf cop from Van Nuys, is behind the wheel. I smile at him. He doesn't smile back. I cross the street.

"What are you doing here?" I ask.

"Get lost," he growls.

"Looking for anyone special?" I ask.

"Take a hike," he says. This is synonymous with 'Get lost'.

"Is this vigil part of your investigation or are you checking out the local beefcake?"

He glares at me searching for a third synonym. He finds it.

"Beat it," he says.

I do what I'm told.

Back at the office, I have Glenda Mae ring up Lt. Overton for me. When he comes on the line, I ask him a simple question.

"Hubbell Cox. Where is he?"

"What are you talking about?"

"You said you had a tail on him and now all of a sudden you've staked out the Naked Apollo. I say you've lost him."

"We'll find him," Overton says.

"What happened?"

"He left the Biltmore early this morning, got in a car with Willie and Little Bob. A few minutes later there was a traffic tie up and they scooted down an alley and my guys lost him."

"Had your guys been spotted?"

"I don't think so," Overton says.

"Maybe our theory of a frame is wrong, Lieutenant," I say. "Maybe Cox is just plain stupid."

"Maybe."

"Let me know when you find him," I say. "I have a few questions I want to ask him."

"About what?"

"Just let me know. Please."

And I hang up.

The rest of the afternoon is just as hectic as yesterday. Slowly the press is shifting its sights away from Kazan and focusing on Overton's thus far failed investigation. I am asked a lot of questions that I cannot answer by a lot of people who know I can't answer them. By six o'cock, I've had enough although I really should go down to the set and talk to Brando about Hedda. Naw, it'll keep. Glenda Mae goes home to Beau and I go home to an empty house. I do not stop for groceries and I do not buy a six pack of beer. The moment of truth may be upon me.

136

Dinner is two eggs over easy, canned lima beans, and a toasted bagel. I heat up leftover coffee from this morning and wander into the living room. I turn on the television, plunk myself into my favorite chair and immediately fall asleep. I am rudely awakened by the ringing of the phone. The clock on the wall says 10:05. What idiot is calling me at 10:05? I lift the receiver and make a noise into it.

"Joe?"

I know her voice immediately. I stumble all over myself trying to get to the television to turn it off.

"Hiya, babe," I say. I frown. 10:05. That's 1:05 in New York. "Are you okay?" I ask.

"Sure," Bunny says.

"It's kinda late," I say. "Not for me, but for you."

"School night," she says with a quiet chuckle. "Right?"

"Right."

"Remember when your mama used to say that. Early bed. It's a school night. Remember, Joe?"

"Sure," I say even though I never really had a Mama.

"I just got lonesome to hear your voice," she says.

"I miss you, too," I say.

There's a pause. I'm trying to decide if she's been drinking.

"I just came in from a date. No, not really a date. Somebody from the magazine. A friend. Just a friend."

"That's nice," I say. She's trying to get to something but I don't know quite what.

"We had dinner at Luchows. Honest to God, Joe, I thought we were going to eat Chinese but it's German. Can you believe that? German."

"I'd heard that," I say. She's had a couple but she's still lucid. Another silence.

"I ate deer. I don't ever want to do that again. Who eats deer, for God's sake."

More silence.

"Joe, I miss you a lot. Do you miss me?"

"Sure, I miss you, Bunny. I wish you were here right now."

"Anthony doesn't mean a thing," she says. "Not a thing. He's very nice but he's just a friend."

"Yes, you said that."

And still more silence.

"Last Saturday we went to the opera. Did you know that Anthony's family has a private box at the Met?"

"I didn't know that."

"We saw Tannhauser. I didn't really understand much of it."

"Wagner's like that," I say.

"I miss you, Joe."

"I miss you, too, Bunny."

"Did I tell you that Anthony's just a friend?"

"You did."

"When we're together after a date at his place or maybe here, I think mostly of you. It's really not the same, Joe. Not the way it was with us. He's just a friend."

I feel a chill come over me. I don't want to hear any more of this.

"Did I wake you up?" she asks. "I'm sorry if I did. I just wanted to tell you that I miss you and I wish you were here." I can hear her choke up and I know she is crying.

"Bunny, don't cry. It's okay."

"It's not okay, Joe," she snuffles. "Nothing's okay."

"Sure, it is, Bunny. We'll be seeing each other in a few weeks."

"Are you sure, Joe? Are you sure you want to see me?"

"Sure, I do."

"He's just a friend, Joe. That's all he is. I promise."

"Okay, why don't you try to get some sleep."

"Sleep. Yes, sleep. I need sleep," she says.

"I love you, Bunny. Go to bed," I say as I hang up.

I stare at the carpet for a long time and then the tears start, just a few in the beginning and then I can't stop them.

CHAPTER FOURTEEN

ou Cioffi , the Times crime reporter, has the story and it's been splashed all over page one of the Wednesday morning edition.

DEVIANT LOVER MAY BE TREMAYNE KILLER.

It's all there. The parked car. The Smoke House parking lot. The lowered trousers. The matchbook from Naked Apollo. Cioffi walks a tightrope to keep it in good taste. The Times is still a family newspaper but he has all the facts. The arrow of suspicion points even further away from both Kazan and Annie Petrakis. They never had much on her to begin with. Now they have even less. I won't be surprised if she's released by the end of the day.

I've been reading this in my kitchen, drinking freshly brewed coffee. Now I pick up the phone and call the Times. I ask for Lou Cioffi. Lou and I go back a couple of years and we've become pretty good friends, at least on a professional level. On my recommendation he was hired as a technical consultant on a film about a crusading crime reporter. Since then I've always been able to get through and this morning is no exception.

"You held out on me, amigo," he says but there's no anger and I can hear the laugh in his tone.

"Who told you that?" I say.

"Lt. Overton who asked me four times if I got my story from you and four times I had to swear on the name of the Blessed Mother that I had not."

"Well, you know if I hadn't been sworn to secrecy, I'd have given it to you first thing."

"I'll pretend to believe you," Lou says. "Anyway, this pretty much clears Kazan."

"I'd say so. So, Lou, where did you get it?"

"Don't know, Joe. My phone rings. A guy who won't reveal his name starts talking, gives me everything the cops have been sitting on. He even tells me the name of the Smoke House security guard who found the body so I'd have corroboration."

"You think it was a cop that tipped you?"

"If I had to bet, I'd say it was the perp. He knew too much too well and never once stuttered. I also think he was disguising his voice."

"But you have no idea who it was?"

"None."

"Hubbell Cox maybe?" I suggest.

"No. I interviewed Cox. Very Texas. The guy on the phone was soft spoken, very educated, and used a lot of big words."

"Somebody from the Naked Apollo?"

"Makes sense to me," Lou says. "By the way, I hear they lost him."

"Cox?"

"Who else?"

"And they still haven't found him?"

"Not to my knowledge," Lou says. "Mighty curious behavior for a man who claims to be innocent."

"Indeed it is," I say as I let Lou get back to work.

On the way to the studio I dial my radio to the news and there it is, basically a rehash of Lou's front page story without giving him credit. Par for the course. Like Lou the radio reporter chooses his words carefully. This is a hell of a story to report accurately without getting down in the gutter.

I pull into my parking spot just as Jack Warner comes by, walking briskly toward the commissary. He waves at me with a broad smile.

"Morning, Joe," he says. "Looks like the fairy son of a bitch got what was coming to him." Jack Warner does not choose his words carefully.

Upstairs Charlie Berger is in a rare mood. Kazan and Warners are no longer connected to this grizzly murder. Charlie is so happy he does not once mention the cost of tuition or the price tags on little girls' clothes.

When I finally get to my office, Glenda Mae gives me a grin and a thumbs up as she says, "Mr. Giordano called. He says good news." I thumbs-up back at her.

"Get him," I say.

When he comes on the phone, he doesn't waste any time.

"Annie's getting out this morning. She should be released by noon."

"Terrific," I say. "It was a lousy collar from the beginning."

"Sure was," Ray says. "Even lousier now that they've caught up with Hub Cox in Tijuana."

"You're kidding."

"Nabbed him late last night in a cantina throwing money around like an oil baron with twenty-four hours to live. Overton's no dummy. When he couldn't find Cox in L.A. he faxed the big cities in northern Mexico just in case. Bingo."

"And what's with the money?"

"No idea but I hear it's close to fifty thousand dollars."

"Being Tremayne's toady seems to have paid very well," I say.

"Maybe so," Ray replies, "but it won't help. Overton's prepping a fugitive warrant and if they can find a judge to issue it, they'll be going down to pick him up, late today or tomorrow."

"I didn't know he was wanted."

"Well, that's part of the problem. Since no charges were ever filed, he technically isn't a fugitive which maybe means no warrant," Ray says. "Gotta run, buddy. I'll let you know when I have Annie safely out on the street."

"Do that," I say and hang up.

I lean back in my chair and sip some coffee from the mugful Glenda Mae brought me while I was on the phone. I'm relaxed and a lot more sanguine than I was a couple of hours ago. And yet, a piece of me is still bothered. I'm pretty sure Hubbell Cox didn't kill Bryce Tremayne. I'm also pretty sure that Overton agrees with me. Apparently we are a minority of two. Granted, Cox makes a good killer. He's homosexual. His past abuse at the hands of Tremyne gives him a motive. The matchbook could be considered damning. He probably had opportunity. It's a perfect wrap up right out of a screenwriter's typewriter. Mystery neatly solved, wrapped up in foil and topped with a ribbon. Story over. Wait expectantly for the next big scandal. Life goes on.

No, I don't buy it and if he's any kind of a cop, neither does Overton. There's something going on here and we don't see it. Not yet. And now as I sit here, puzzled, I think to myself, 'Idiot! What is wrong with you? Kazan and Annie have been cleared, This is not your problem any more.' Even if I gave a damn about Bryce Tremayne, which I don't, I would still be saying to myself, 'This is none of your damned business.'

For the first time in days I think I have my priorities straight and I feel so good I decide to visit the set to talk to Brando. I am thinking about the five bucks Charlie will soon be handing me.

The red light over the stage door is off so I enter the sound stage where they are setting up for the next shot. As I recall it's a one on one. Stanley and Blanche. Vivien Leigh is nowhere to be seen and is likely in her dressing room. Brando and Kazan are camped on chairs, heads together, looking over the script. Kazan looks up with a smile and greets me. Brando turns toward me and grins.

"Hey, Joe. Nice goin', man. How do you like that guy Tremayne? Is that something or what?" Brando says shaking his head.

"Hard to believe," I say.

"Big shots," he says. "The bigger they are the more they got to hide. You think about it, Joe. I'm right about that." He turns to Kazan. "Am I right, Gadge?"

"If you say so, Bud," Kazan says.

At that moment, the assistant director comes over and whispers in Kazan's ear. He glowers and then gets up. "Excuse me, gentlemen, there are some feathers that need unruffling." He walks off.

Brando watches him go with a sour expression. "A saint. The man's a saint."

"Trouble?" I ask.

"If you were to inquire, I would tell you that a certain person, and I will not tell you who, needs a fast kick in her butt. England's only got one queen and she ain't it."

"Well, I'm sure Gadge can handle things," I say. "And by the way, don't worry about Hedda Hopper. I took care of her. After I explained things to Mr. Warner, he said he'd run interference for you."

Brando seems confused. "What are you talking about, man?"

"Hedda Hopper. The interview. When she couldn't get Kazan she wanted you and when we refused, she made all kinds of threats, crazy things about your relationship with Kazan and your roommate back in New York, Wally Cox, and you know, Bud, it's the usual crap. We knew you couldn't handle her so we went to bat for you."

Brando scowls at me. "What do you mean, who couldn't handle who? What are you talking about?"

I smile. "Oh, come on, Bud, she's been doing this stuff for years. She's a shark. She'd run rings around you. We couldn't have that."

Now Brando is insulted. "Excuse me, my friend, but I think I am a good judge of what I can handle and what I cannot and I will tell you that given the chance I could turn that nosy bitch into cat food."

I shake my head. "No, no. Don't even think about it. Bud."

"And very frankly, Joe, I am disappointed in you because I do not appreciate the studio blowing my nose for me, do you understand? Now if this woman wants to interview me, I say let's do it. Anytime and any place."

"Bud, I really don't think---"

"No, please, do not think, Joe. Just set it up. I would take it as a personal favor."

I sigh helplessly. "All right, if you're sure---"

He smiles. "I'm sure and I thank you for worrying about me but I am a big boy and I know the score."

I leave the soundstage having told Brando that I will let him know as soon as we have a firm meeting date with Hopper. Then I will go to my office, call Hedda with the good news and then go to Charlie's office where I will try valiantly to feign humility while I relieve him of a five dollar bill.

Back at the office I get on the phone with Hedda who is delighted by the news. I have made Brownie points with her by proving I am a man of my word although they may quickly disappear if Brando is actually able to make cat food out of her. While Hedda and I are chatting a call comes in for me and when I hang up, Glenda Mae tells me that Jennifer Coughlin called and left a number. I'm intrigued.

"Hi," I say when she answers the phone.

"Hi, yourself," she says. "I called to tell you I moved out of the Biltmore."

"That's not all you moved out of," i say.

"Oh, you must have talked with Elvira."

"I did."

"I guess she said I was fired."

"Words to that effect."

"No problem. I was going to quit anyway."

"More time for the book?"

"You bet," she says. "Joe, do you remember the last time we chatted I said I hadn't given up on you."

"I remember."

"How about coming by this evening? I'll ply you with booze and cook you dinner and after that, we'll play it by ear."

"I could handle that," I say. "Where are you?"

She gives me an address which is near the top of Laurel Canyon Boulevard on the Beverly Hills side. A friend from her UCLA days rents there and invited her to move in temporarily. The friend is a Pan Am stewardess and at the moment she's in Rome. We'll have the place to ourselves. She has made me an offer that a week ago I could have refused but after last night's call from Bunny, I accept. After all, Jennifer is just a friend.

Shortly before seven o'clock I find myself climbing Laurel

Canyon, looking for the little side street that shoots off to the right. Just when I think I might have missed it, there it is. I turn and pass five houses on my left hand side and then turn into a wide driveway per her instructions. At the end of the driveway, I see it. It's a small, nicely kept one story guest cottage. The lights are on and it is welcoming. I park my car next to a late model Buick sedan, go to the door and knock. In a moment she opens it and smiles. It's worth repeating that this is a gorgeous smile and I am now very glad that I accepted this invitation. She leans forward and brushes a friendly kiss on my cheek as I step inside.

It is small but warm and cozy with a fireplace that has been lit. Standing by the fireplace is a man whose back is toward me. I am surprised because I thought this was to be dinner for two.

The man is of average height and average build and when he turns to face me, I see that his face is deeply tanned and that he boasts a full head of white hair and a neatly trimmed white bushy mustache.

CHAPTER FIFTEEN

The man steps away from the hearth and approaches me, a drink in his left hand, right hand extended and a smile on his face.

"Good evening, Mr. Bernardi. At long last we meet. Jed Tompkins," he says. He speaks authentic Texan but it isn't larded with pone the way Tremayne used to talk. I also know who he is. J. Farrell Tompkins is Elvira's father and one of the richest and most powerful ranchers in south Texas. His grip is firm but not intimidating and he exudes down home warmth.

"How do you do, Mr. Tompkins?" I say.

"That's Jed, son. Jedidiah. A name given by the prophet Nathan to Solomon, the wise king. My mother loved her Bible and I guess she thought the name would make me a smart fella."

"I'd say she was probably right," I say politely.

"There are those who would disagree," he says. "I just fixed myself a drink. What can I get you?"

"I'm a beer drinker, Jed," I say.

"We can accomodate that," he says. "Jenny." He nods toward the improvised bar set up against the wall. Jenny quickly goes to it and finds me a beer. It isn't Coors but I don't complain.

Tompkins gestures toward the sofa. "Sit down, Joe. Let's you and me get acquainted." He sits and I join him. As I do, I throw Jenny a look and he catches it. "Don't go blaming Jenny for this. My idea. And don't fret about your dinner plans. I won't be staying long."

I nod with a smile. "How did you like Chasen's restaurant Friday evening?" I ask.

"Loved the food. Can't say the same for the company," he says.

"I suppose you two had a lot to discuss," I say.

"No, son, Bryce Tremayne and me never had much to chat about."

"Then you didn't care much for his politics."

"That, too, but mostly I didn't care much for Bryce Tremayne. I found him to be shallow, egotistical, dishonest, an ignorant blowhard and a piece of human debris not fit to be married to my daughter."

"Yet you had dinner with him."

"He was the one who extended the invitation. At my daughter's insistence, I accepted. Elvira made a serious mistake years ago, Joe. She and I both knew it right from the git-go. Hell, son, everybody knew it but she could not bring herself to admit she had been wrong."

I look around and Jenny has disappeared from the room, probably on orders from this man. Whatever I thought this evening might be, it's now plain I was misled.

"And you've been in town how long?"

"A few days," he says.

"And you came to Los Angeles because----" I let it hang.

"Years ago when they were first married, Bryce took liberties with Elvira. Even if she were not my daughter I have no use for a man who strikes a woman and so I warned him that if he ever did it again, I would destroy him. He took me at my word until a couple of weeks ago. Willie Babbitt called me and told me what happened. I flew in that evening. When I saw Bryce it was all I could do to keep myself from striking him. Of course, he was apologetic. It would never happen again, he said. He practically fell to his knees begging my forgiveness and of course, I forgave him. Those words were for public consumption. Privately I had other plans for Bryce Tremayne."

"And now we know what they were," I say.

He almost laughs. "Surely you cannot think me that stupid. Murder? And a clumsy and degrading one at that. No, no, Joe, when I set my sights on a man, my methods are far less public and far more devastating. I was going to turn him into an inconsequential nothing, despised instead of beloved, mocked instead of feared and it would all have been perfectly legal."

I nod sagely. "Jedidiah, the wise," I say. "And so, Jedidiah, the big question. Why are you telling me all this?"

"Very simply to save myself some unneeded embarrassment. I came to the city sub rosa, checked into a small hotel under an alias and kept a low profile. I am considering a run for the United States Senate next year and I want to keep my personal life as unsullied as possible. Having dinner with a son in law I despise and then having that son in law discovered murdered in such a disgusting manner within a matter of hours puts me in a situation I need to avoid."

I shake my head. "You can't really expect to keep your presence in the city at the time of his death a secret," I say.

"I do and so far, I have."

"Yes, two of your persuaders came by my house the other evening," I say.

He nods thoughtfully. "That was a mistake."

"I'll say."

"I'm sorry, Joe. It shouldn't have happened. Subtlety is not a part of Willie Babbitt's make up. He violated my instructions and all I can do is fervently apologize. It's not enough but it will have to do. In any case I am a rich man with many friends. I can be a valuable ally for you at such time that you need one. All I ask is that you do and say nothing to involve me. I am going back to San Antonio tomorrow and taking Elvira with me. As far as I am concerned, that will close the matter."

"I doubt Lt. Overton would agree."

"Tread carefully, Joe," he says. His expression hardens.

"Overton's not a fool. If you have nothing to hide, you'll be all right."

"A Senate candidate with rumors of murder hanging over him will not be all right."

He stands up and looks down at me. "Be practical, Joe. Do the smart thing. I can be a very, very good friend."

Now I get up and look him in the eye.

"I guess I'm not smart, Jed, and I have more very good friends than I know what to do with."

He hesitates for the longest time and then he says, "I admire a man who stands by his principles no matter what the outcome." There's an iciness in his demeanor as he puts out his hand and we shake again. "Convey my regards to Jennifer," he says. "I'll find my way out."

He walks to the door and leaves. I hear his car start up and then drive away. I turn back into the room to see Jenny standing in the open bedroom doorway, watching me intently.

"I'm sorry, Joe. I didn't have a choice."

"Looks like everybody takes orders from J. Farrell Tompkins. How long have you been working for him?"

"From the beginning," she says. "He's a minority stock-holder in a publishing company based in Houston."

"I see. So the hatchet job on Tremayne was his idea."

"No, it was mine but he jumped at it. I get the dirt on Tremayne, all the sordid little deals, how he uses extortion and blackmail to get information, his secret sex life, the fantasy past he's invented for himself. Get it all and get it documented and the book gets published. A tell all that'll shoot to number one and make Jenny a rich little girl. That's how he put it. I couldn't miss."

She walks over to the bar and pours herself a Jack Daniels neat. Three fingers worth and drains it in one long swallow.

"How'd you feel about it?" I ask.

"Shitty," she says. "Bryce was a poor excuse for a human being but it didn't take me long to realize I was not much better."

"I doubt that."

She puts the empty glass down on the bar and very care-fully refills it, this time almost to the top. "Thanks for saying it, Joe, but it doesn't help. Self-awareness is high up on my list of traits." She walks toward me. "Look, you don't have to stick around to watch me get drunk. Go home to that girl who has you sort of spoken for."

"She's in New York," I say.

"Well, that's stupid of her," Jenny says, taking a swallow of her drink.

"Job oppoprtunity," I say. "She works for Colliers Magazine as a sort of assistant editor."

"Goody for her," Jenny says. "Does she work twenty four hours a day or does she find time for diversion? We women need diversion, Joe. Take it from me. I know."

"Bunny likes her fun," I say.

She chuckles. "Bunny. Cute, Joe. Funny, too. You know what bunnies do, Joe? They do it a lot. I'll bet you can't guess."

She's put her drink down on a table and now she's close to me. Very close. She slips her hands under the lapels of my sport jacket and pulls me toward her and then she is softly kissing my neck, exploring with her tongue. For a moment I am frozen and then I feel my arms encircling her and pulling her close to me. She is soft and smells of rosewater and I feel a stirring below my belt buckle that I cannot control even if I wanted to. She's aware of it, too, and she looks up at me and our lips move together and I am drinking her in. Soft little noises are coming from her throat as my hands move down across her buttocks and she searches with her tongue. Her hand slips down toward my crotch, searching and rubbing and I am getting dizzy. I can't stop and yet I know I must and I reach down and grab her wrist very tightly and stop her.

She looks at me wide-eyed. "What's the matter?"

"Nothing. Everything. I can't."

"Joe, it doesn't mean anything," she says, her voice husky with passion.

"I know," I say. "That's the problem."

She speaks quietly. I can barely hear her. "Do you know how long it's been since I've made love to someone I cared about?"

I gently extricate myself from her embrace and look into her eyes. Whatever it is she's doing, she's not faking it.

"I'm sorry," I say. She looks away. "I can't explain it. I won't even try.

She looks back at me, not understanding.

"I'd better leave," I say. I go to the door. She follows me. I open it and look down at her.

"Rain check?" I say.

"No rain in the forecast, Joe."

I nod. "My loss," I say. "Good night, Jenny."

I walk out into the night to my car. She watches me from the doorway and then slowly closes the door.

I slip behind the wheel of my car and close the door but I don't start the engine. I stare straight ahead into the darkened woods that abut the cottage. I wonder what in hell is the matter with me. Bunny has drifted so far away I may never get her back and even so I harbor delusions of happily ever after. Delusions. It's a good word. Bunny is becoming more and more a fantasy and Jenny Coughlin is flesh and blood. Have I just been steadfast and noble or just plain stupid? Should I walk back in there and put an end to this bicoastal nightmare once and for all? I probably should but I can't bring myself to do it. Yes, I am a fool and there's no help for me.

I start the engine, flip on the lights and start out of the driveway. It's past nine-thirty and it is quiet. The denizens of Beverly Hills, at least these hilltoppers, are early to bed. I see a light on here and there but no one is really stirring and there is no traffic. There are also no street lights so I keep the speed to a minimum on the winding downhill narrow lane. I look into my rear view mirror as a pickup truck emerges from a side street and slips in behind me. It seems odd to me that a pickup truck would be roaming around this neighborhood at this time of night but I don't have much time to ruminate about it. The truck speeds up and slams viciously into my back bumper.

I swerve badly but manage to regain control as my headlights search for the road ahead. The street is barely two car widths wide and a bad skid will put me into a ditch or into the woods or onto someone's front lawn. The truck roars upon me again and deliberately slams into the left side of my bumper and I see what he is trying to do, to put me into a wild spin where I will have no control. I fight the wheel even as my headlights pick up a four foot stone wall dead ahead. I yank the wheel to the right and and barely pull out of a head-on crash as the wall scrapes across the left side of the car.

I'm starting to sweat. I'm a lousy driver and I know it and the guy behind me seems to know exactly what he is doing. I would like to lean on the car horn to attract attention and maybe scare him off but I need both hands on the wheel to maintain control. A yellow and black sign with an arrow is coming up on my right. It shows a sharp left turn with a speed limit of 10 mph. I'm doing 35 and can't afford to slow down. The truck bears down on me again and again slams into my left bumper. I can feel myself losing it. I glance into the rear view and for a fleeting moment I think I see flashing red lights way back up the road. And then I've lost it. I'm off the pavement and jouncing downward into a vacant lot. I think I hit a large rock and nearly go onto my side as the tires fight for a grip in the heavy long grass. A tree looms up in front of me. I can't avoid it. I brace myself on the steering wheel as I collide. My head snaps forward but stops short of the windshield and I fall back into my seat. The car is now motionless. The engine has cut out.

For a few moments I sit very still. It is quiet again and I'm aware that I'm breathing hard and my heart is pumping like the rat-a-tat-tat of a tommy gun. Out of the corner of my left eye I am aware of a blinking red light and I look up toward the roadway where a car is stopped. A single red light sits on its roof. I can see a man coming down the incline, struggling to keep his balance as he heads toward me. I find the window handle and roll it down as he reaches the car. It's Shorty, the diminutive cop from the Van Nuys Division, and for once I am glad to see him.

CHAPTER SIXTEEN

"No, we weren't watching the girl," Overton says. "We decided to keep an eye on you."

"Thanks. Now I'm back to being a suspect," I say.

We are once again sitting in the office of W.W. Reilly, Commander of the Van Nuys Division, who is once again nowhere to be seen. It's ten thirty at night and the selfish fellow is probably at home with his family and most likely, tucked into bed getting some shut eye. I, on the other hand, am having to deal with officialdom but since officialdom may have just saved my life, I decide not to whine about it.

"No, Mr. Bernardi, you are not a suspect but you are, however, often at the center of developments that are really none of your business. For that reason alone you deserve our attention. And by the way, a word of thanks to Detective Silvestri would not be out of place."

"You mean Shorty?"

"He prefers Silvestri."

"You're right and I will thank him."

"Good," Overton says, "and now that you have been snatched from the jaws of death, how about sharing what you've been so desperately trying to hide for the past few days. Think of it as a small favor in return for saving your worthless life."

I shrug. "Well, since you put it that way---." I have a hot mug of coffee in front of me and I take a swig. I've already downed a glass of water and four aspirin to deal with the aches and pains that are suddenly starting to show up post-trauma.

"For starters," I say, "the widow Tremayne's father is in town. His name is J. Farrell Tompkins and he's richer than God and twice as powerful."

"We know about Mr. Tompkins," Overton says.

"Did you know that he had dinner with the victim only a few hours before Tremayne was found dead in the Smoke House parking lot?"

Overton has a pretty good poker face but he couldn't hide this one. He hadn't a clue. "Tell me," he says.

"They ate at Chasen's. Maybe eight o'clock to nine-thirty. I have no idea what they talked about and Tompkins isn't saying. But more importantly he doesn't want anyone to know he was there. J. Farrell has political ambitions and while it was bad enough having Tremayne for a son-in-law, buying him Beef Wellington at a clandestine meeting a few hours before he was iced is a sure vote loser."

"You're sure of this?"

"Annie Petrakis saw him though she didn't know who he was. Also Alice, the cocktail waitress. They both can pick him out of a lineup. As for Luis, the waiter, he suddenly developed a need to see his mother in Mexico City and I don't think it was a spontaneous decision. And oh yes, when Alice described Tremayne's guest to Hubbell Cox and me, Hubbell nearly swallowed his bridgework. Another little piece for your jigsaw puzzle." I smile. "By the way, how is old Hubbell? I hear you've got him safely salted away in a Tijuana jail cell."

"We did," Overton says.

"Ooops," I say.

"He slipped away about four hours ago. The Tijuana police are scouring the city for him."

"Think they'll find him?"

"Depends on how hard they look. When they arrested him, they impounded all his cash."

"I get it. They have his money. They don't need him. In fact it's even better if he just disappears and is never seen or heard from again."

"Not a good situation for Hubbell," Overton says.

"Not good at all," I echo. "So what do you think?" I ask.

"You mean, did he do it?" Overton replies. He leans back in W.W. Reilly's leather covered desk chair and stares at the ceiling for a few moments. "The facts add up to a probable yes," he says, "but my cop brain says no. I have to admit, though, his running like that, it doesn't look good."

My press agent brain also says no, but Overton is right. Cox's flight across the border raises a lot of questions.

"What about extradition?" I ask.

Overton shrugs. "Technically he's not a fugitive. He was never charged."

"But I'll bet you could get a warrant if you really tried."

"Maybe so," Overton says, "but that presupposes we can find him and that the Tijuana cops will actually help rather than hinder in the search and finally, that the Mexican government will cooperate. When a possible death sentence is in play, they can create mountains of red tape."

"And if you don't find him and bring him back, if he just melts into the Mexican countryside?"

"Then assumptions will be made about his guilt, the

newspapers will lose interest and the case will slip between the cracks."

"And the real killer will live happily ever after," I say.

"This is real life, Mr. Bernardi," Overton says. "Sometimes the lady with the scales goes on a coffee break."

"Don't tell John Wayne," I say. "The thought would crush him."

Overton smiles and I think he's not such a bad guy after all. To prove it, he arranges transportation home. Shorty gets to do the honors and I keep my promise by using his proper name and thanking him profusely for saving my life. By the time we pull into the driveway we are laughing and scratching like two old frat brothers who haven't seen each other in years. He even shows me a picture of his wife who is a real looker but towers over him like a lamppost. I hold my tongue as he drives away with a cheery wave.

Morning comes much too quickly. The cops have pulled my damaged Ford out of the weed patch and stashed it at their impound. I call my insurance guy first thing in the morning and he tells me not to worry. He'll arrange to have it towed to the dealer and a claims adjuster will be out before noon to take a look. Meantime, do I need a loaner? I say no because Bunny's beat up Plymouth is in the garage. There's a moment of trepidation as I turn the key but even though it's been sitting unused for a couple of months, it kicks in right away.

By the time i get to the office I realize that everybody's got the latest news. I hear it from the radio guy first and once I'm in my office I start to read Lou Cioffi's page one story.

FUGITIVE SUSPECT SOUGHT BY MEXICAN POLICE

That says it all but there are a few details I wasn't aware of. Cox was originally picked up in a cantina in a state of drunken revelry. They'd been tipped by an anonymous phone call that he'd slipped into the country unobserved so the cops were on the lookout. I wonder who this anonymous good citizen was. The police find a huge amount of money on him but as to exactly how much, no one is sure. He was locked up in a small cell in the back of the police station but little attention was paid to him. At eight o'clock someone walked back to check on him and found the cell door wide open and Cox missing. No one at the station has a really good explanation as to how this might have happened. A search gets underway. So far, no sign of him.

I consider the worst case scenario. The cops, now in possession of his cash, help him "escape". They take him out to sea and dump him overboard with cement booties on his feet. There are other methods, equally effective, and all are ugly possibilities. I hope I'm wrong but it would certainly simplify things for the real perpetrator still here in Los Angles and, as yet, unidentified. Again I realize that with Cox a fugitive, the case is more or less solved. No more effort will be expended and in a few months all the "evidence" will be packed in a box and stored in the basement alongside the other cold cases.

I shake my head. I tell myself once again that none of this is my affair. And yet, I keep getting sucked into the middle of this muddle. Today is Thursday, the fourth day of shooting. I have visited the set exactly twice. I have not yet met Kim Hunter which is a terrible breach of protocol. I have not attended any screenings of the rushes though I hear they look wonderful. It is time, I say to myself for the fiftieth time in a week, to get back to work.

The call comes in at 1:24. Glenda Mae is lunching with a couple of her female buddies, one of which has just gotten engaged. I don't expect her back until at least three o'clock and it's a probable seven to five that she'll be reasonably sober.

I lift the receiver.

"Bernardi."

"Joe? Thank God."

I recognize his voice immediately.

"Hubbell? Where the hell are you?"

"Mexico," he says.

"The whole damned world knows that. Where in Mexico?"

He doesn't answer my question. "Joe, you have to help me. I don't know who else I can turn to. Or who else I can trust."

"Hubbell, I'd like to help you but---"

"I didn't kill him, Joe. I swear to God. You have to believe me. I didn't do it."

"I believe you," I say.

There's a pause. "You do?"

"I believe you and so does Lt.Overton but you have to come back."

"I want to." There's desperation in his voice. "I can't stay here, Joe. They're trying to kill me."

"Who is?"

"The cops. The three cops who arrested me and got my money. Most of it, anyway."

"Well, what did you expect when you get drunk In some cantina and start throwing a lot of greenbacks around?"

"No, no!" he says sharply. "Who told you that? I was sitting in a little restaurant next to the Jai AlaI fronton drinking coffee and trying to decide my next move when these three guys grabbed me and took my overnight bag with most of my cash in it."

"Fifty thousand dollars," I say.

"Who have you been talking to? Nothing like that. Ten thousand maybe. Enough to get me to Mexico City and catch on with some outfit that could use a bilingual executive."

"Okay, Hubbell, slow down and start over. How did you get to Mexico? Where did the money come from? Why did you run?"

"I ran because the old man was trying to frame me for Bryce's murder. Hell, Joe, as soon as I heard the cocktail girl's description, I realized J.T. was in the city and I knew why. Because Bryce had popped Elvira one too many times. I went back to the Biltmore to see if I could track him down. Elvira wouldn't tell me where he was but she said the cops were ready to arrest me at any moment. They had my fingerprints and they'd been following me around. even into the Naked Apollo where they had somebody undercover. Oh, hell, Joe, I guess I'd had a snootful too many times and I'd get started on what a prick Bryce was and how he'd screwed me over and how I'd like to kill the son of a bitch. Drunk talk, you know what I mean. But I'd said it and I knew how it looked."

"And running looked like your best option."

"Elvira felt bad for me but also grateful for what I'd done even though I denied it vehemently. She had a lot of cash on hand and she gave it to me. She knew I spoke fluent Spanish and that I could make a new start in Mexico. Willie volunteered to drive me to the border so I wouldn't have to use public transportation in case they were watching the trains and the busses. At two o'clock in the morning I walked across without a hitch."

"And the next day you got picked up on a tip. You ever wonder where that tip might have come from?"

"Somebody reading the L.A. papers, maybe," he says.

"You give your fellow man a lot of credit," I say.

"Meaning that the call could have come from Elvira or Jed Tompkins or Willie or even Little Bob? I don't think so," Cox says.

"Good," I say. "You keep that thought. Maybe you'll be lucky and it won't kill you."

"No, you're wrong, Joe, but I know I have to come back. Will you help me?"

"The Los Angeles police will help you."

"I don't trust them either."

"You're pretty fussy for a guy being hunted like a wounded deer. Where are you?"

"Ensenada. I'm holed up in a room in a house near the pier. I darkened my hair and I'm wearing sunglasses. No one knows who I am. I figure if you could rent a fishing boat in San Pedro and from there, it's only about seventy five miles down the coast. You pull up to the pier, I hop on, we head back to the states and I turn myself in."

"What about the Ensenada cops?"

"I haven't seen any," he says.

I hesitate. I'd like to help the guy because I think he's being screwed over royally. But Overton's right. I keep sticking my nose where it has no right to be. And besides I don't have the time. Good arguments. Persuasive. I'd be a fool to keep getting involved in this mess.

"All right, I'll see what I can do," I say defying my own logic, "but if I do this, the cops are in on it."

"No."

"Yes, Hubbell. No cops, no me. You're a fugitive. If I help you on my own I'm an accomplice and I could be looking at serious jail time."

"But---"

"No buts. Take it or leave it."

There's a long silence and then he reluctantly agrees.

"How can I get in touch with you?" I ask.

"You can't," he says. "I'm at a pay phone."

"All right," I say, "call me back at four o'clock. That'll give me time to put this together. If we come it'll be after dark."

He agrees and I hang up.

I immediately call Overton and tell him what's going on. When I'm finished, he says, "We'll pick him up. You stay out of it."

"Won't work,"I say. "He doesn't trust you guys. If he doesn't see me, he'll run for it."

"Damn it, Bernardi, you're a civilian."

"And don't I know it. Tell you what, Lieutenant, when he calls in at four I'll tell him I'm out of the picture and we'll see how long it takes for him to hang up."

Overton hesitates. "Okay. We do it your way."

"Fine, Give me one guy. I don't want to chug into that port with half the LAPD on board."

"All right. It'll be just the two of us," Overton says.

"No," I say. "You seem like a good guy, Lieutenant, but I want somebody on my back I know I can count on."

"And that somebody would be?"

"Aaron Kleinschmidt."

"Why am I not surprised by that? All right. I'll ask him. He'll have to volunteer."

I laugh. "Bullshit. Just tell him. He's a good cop. He loves to be ordered around."

"Let me explain something to you, Mr. Bernardi," Overton says after a moment's hesitation. "I will be asking one of my men who has no jurisdiction beyond the borders of the City of Los Angles to sneak into the sovereign nation of Mexico and illegally extradite a fugitive from justice without notifying any official personage, not even their postmaster general. People have been shot for less."

"Well put, Lieutenant. Call me back and let me know what he says," I say.

"If he finds out you're involved and if he has any brains at all, I can tell you what he'll say."

Overton is wrong. He says that Aaron is delighted to be a part of this operation. He looks forward to it. The fact that I will be tagging along only makes it more challenging.

CHAPTER SEVENTEEN

We're in an unmarked cop car and driving south on Figueroa Street toward the San Pedro harbor. Aaron Kleinschmidt is driving. I volunteered Bunny's Plymouth but he took one look and immediately called the motor pool. As for my Ford, the insurance adjuster tells me it is a total wreck and not worth repairing. The company will honor my claim and mail me a check for about 50% of the car's value. Immediately upon returning to L.A. I will buy a new car and find myself another insurance company.

As we pass through the less desirable sections of Carson and Wilmington, we get a lot of nasty stares. How is it that even seven year olds know an unmarked cop car when they see it? We get lucky and nobody throws anything at us and we pull into the pier area of San Pedro shortly after five o'clock.

We go in search of a San Pedro police officer named Esteban Rodriguez and a 22' Chris Craft custom sedan cruiser named "Paradiso". We have gotten lucky. Overton has arranged for us to use this classy speedboat which was confiscated several months ago by the San Pedro cops from its previous owner who is now awaiting trial on charges of importing proscribed goods without a license and conducting his business in the dead of night away from the prying eyes of the local authorities and the U.S. Coast Guard.

We find Esteban at the end of a pier in swim trunks and a tee shirt hosing down the boat. He gives a friendly wave as we approach. I understand that he, too, is looking forward to tonight's adventure. I mean, how many parking tickets can you hand out without going out of your mind? It's a package deal. Esteban comes with the boat or no boat. We don't mind. Aaron and I are landlubbers. We know from nothing about celestial navigation and the care and maintenance of high powered engines.

By five-thirty we leave San Pedro harbor. The arrangements are these. We expect to reach Ensenada around eleven. It will be dark and the harbor will be fairly quiet. The fishing boats will all be moored and the fishermen home with their families until daybreak tomorrow. Hubbell Cox has bought a powerful flashlight and some red cellophane which he will wrap around the lens. He will wave the light slowly back and forth so we can locate him. We will pull up to the pier, he will climb aboard and we will scoot back to San Pedro. This is contingent on nothing going wrong. We remain optimistic even though we have it on good authority that Murphy's Law was invented by law enforcement. This is why both Aaron and Esteban are packing heat. As for my .25 caliber Beretta I left it home figuring it would be pretty useless in an all out fire fight.

The larder is filled with sandwiches and soda and we break out something to eat and watch the seaside towns go by on our port side. This gives us plenty to talk about but when the sun finally slips below the horizon and the sky turns dark, the chit chat stops. There are only occasional lights to be seen on shore. We're way past San Diego and when we see brighter lights in the sky up ahead, Esteban tells us we'll soon be in Mexican waters, passing Tijuana. After that it won't be long to Ensenada.

Esteban warns that from time to time La Guardacostos Mexicana puts in an appearance. We'll try to avoid them but if we can't, we'll just pretend to be three stupid gringos out for a midnight cruise who have no idea where they are. I tell Esteban no problem. I can do stupid with the best of them.

The sun has been down for well over an hour and a chill has descended over the boat. Although the sky is clear, the sliver of a crescent moon provides little illumination and the dark and the dampness are starting to get to me. I sit on the deck, arms clasped around my body as I huddle seeking warmth. The silence is broken only by the occasional clang of a buoy marker, the sloshing of the ocean waters against the hull and the guttural sound of the twin engines as the boat knifes southward toward our destination. I look up at Esteban at the wheel, his eyes piercing the darkness ahead. There is a set to his jaw that I recognize. I saw it many times in the fields and on the roads of France and Western Germany, the look of warriors anticipating battle and prepared for whatever was to come. Aaron Kleinschmidt, staring out over the inky Pacific waters, shares the expression. An odd feeling comes over me. I realize there is danger ahead but I am not afraid. Nervous, yes. Frightened, no.

It occurs to me that I am not here out of some misbegotten sense of duty but because I want to be here. I harken back to the Oklahoma oil fields when I would be working on a rig and a ferocious windstorm would loom up out of nowhere threatening life and limb. And that day in France when my driver took a wrong turn and we found ourselves in the middle of a German counterattack, alternately running and hiding , desperately trying to make our way back to the Allied lines, wallowing in mud and diving into ditches and then leaping into the air in exultation when we were discovered by a G.I.scouting party.

Time and again in my youth I was tested and not found wanting and now I am a thirty one year old man who sits at a typewriter and ballyhoos movies and mollycoddles friends and enemies alike. The adventure that was my youth is over and while I would not go out of my way to relive it, in many ways I miss it. I shift position and lift my head to stare out over the water. The salty spry of the ocean slaps me in the face and I feel very much alive.

A short time later I feel the boat start to slow and veer toward port and when I look I can see the port of Ensenada looming up ahead. As it turns out, the Mexican coast guard boys were busy elsewhere and at eleven oh six, we turn slowly into the harbor and start looking for Cox's signal.

Our engines are turning just fast enough to keep from stalling out as we glide almost noiselessly past the fishing boats, anchored side by side by side. Here and there we pass an older pleasure boat, not quite a yacht, and four or five smaller speedboats, fourteen feet long at most. We strain our eyes and for a minute or two I fear the worst. The Tijuana cops may have found him. But no, there's the signal. Esteban sees it first, further ahead and to the right. He tweaks the engines so they speed up ever so slightly. Aaron isn't watching Cox. His eyes are scanning the rest of the harbor, alert to any potential trouble.

Esteban edges our sturdy Chris Craft gently up against the pier as I look into the dark shadows of the weather beaten buildings a hundred feet or so away. And then Cox emerges from the blackness running toward us. At that moment, shadowy figures appear from nowhere and try to run him down before he can reach us. Voices are screaming in Spanish and as I look more closely I think I see three of them.

Aaron grabs a gaff that has been lying on the boat deck and he leaps onto the pier. Esteban shouts for me to grab the wheel and hold steady and as I reach him to grasp the wheel, he makes a dash onto the pier following in Aaron's wake. The boat is fighting me and I'm not good enough to know exactly what to do but even though I am bouncing and jouncing off of the pier I don't let it get away. I look across to the melee and Aaron is slugging one of the three with the handle end of the gaff while Esteban has Cox in tow and is hustling him toward the boat. One of the three men draws a gun and shouts "Policia!" Aaron pulls his own weapon and fires at the man's knee cap. He goes down in a scream of pain as Aaron levels his gun at the other two even as he is backing away toward our boat.

As Esteban hoists Cox onto the boat and follows, Aaron turns and heads toward us at a dead run. I feel Esteban push me out of the way and regain control of the wheel as Aaron vaults onto the deck. I move aside and look to the pier where the wounded man is being tended to by the others. Beneath my feet I feel a huge surge of power as our boat turns and starts to speed toward the harbor entrance. I kneel down next to Cox who is lying on the deck, trying to catch his breath.

"Are you okay?" I ask.

He nods, then says, "Tijuana. They were Tijuana cops. I recognized them."

"Shit!" I hear Esteban yell and I look up. Dead ahead a large cabin cruiser has swung into position in front of us. A huge searchlight is aimed directly at us while a man with a bullhorn is shouting orders in Spanish. The light is blinding and for a moment we are frozen. Then Esteban yells out, "Okay, boys. Up to you. What do we do?"

"Can we outrun them?" Aaron shouts.

"Maybe!"

Aaron looks over at me. I don't hesitate. I nod.

"Let's get the hell out of here!" Aaron yells.

Esteban responds by giving it full power and heading straight for the Mexican boat. He yells to Aaron, "The searchlight!"

Aaron nods and draws his pistol, bracing himself against the railing. We are flying straight toward it and when we are only twenty yards apart, Aaron rips off three quick shots. The searchlight shatters and the cabin cruiser goes blind. Esteban yanks the wheel and we skim by the other boat on its port side, avoiding collision by a matter of feet. I hear shots and one of the slugs buries into the cabin wall next to my head. Esteban turns and looks back, a huge grin on his face, and he extends his middle finger in a gesture of farewell.

As we had passed the other boat, I noticed two things. One, there were no official markings and two, it was bigger than we were and presumably faster. These crooked Tijuana cops are freelancing with the help of some friends and something tells me that if they catch up with us, we won't have to worry about a trial by jury.

I hear excitable voices in the distance, yammering away in Spanish. Then I hear the full throated roar of their engine and I know that the opposition will be in hot pursuit in a matter of moments. I look at Esteban. He doesn't seem worried. Neither does Aaron who kneels down next to me with a smile.

"When you are transporting illegal drugs from port to port, it pays to have the fastest boat on the pond. The former owner made sure that he did."

I look back at him with a smile of understanding.

Within a few minutes, I hear no roar of a competing engine or frustrated cries of anger in Spanish. All I can hear is the whine of our own engine and feel the balmy breeze of the Mexican waters wafting through my hair as we head back home. I'm content, Cox is relieved, and my two cops look like they just had the time of their lives.

It's nearly five o'clock when we drag ourselves back to San Pedro Harbor. We are cold, tired and in bad need of sleep. We are also hungry. The soda and sandwiches ran out a long time ago and when Esteban gets the boat properly tied up he suggests a hot breakfast at a nearby cafe that opens very early for the local fisherman. Aaron and I don't need to be asked twice.

Pancho's is small and badly lit and smells a lot like tomatoes and beans and chili but Esteban promises they serve a terrific huevos rancheros. We take his word for it and even though Mexican food is at the bottom of my eat list, I have to admit Pancho whips up a pretty tasty breakfast. The coffee is even better. We laugh a lot about our adventure now that any real danger is long past. Hubbell thanks us several times for saving his life. All in the line of duty, Aaron says, but we all know that isn't true.

"You know we are going to take you into custody," Aaron says.

"Yes, I understand."

"The Lieutenant is not at all sure you're guilty but for the moment, it's for your own protection until we can get things sorted out," Aaron says.

"Yes, no problem," Cox says. "I appreciate everything you've done for me."

I look over at Cox and say, "Hubbell, you do know that you were set up."

He meets my look and shakes his head. "You said that before, Joe , but you're wrong. Sure, it could have been Jed Tompkins but it wasn't Jed that helped me get to Mexico.It was Elvira and

Willie and Little Bob. And the Tijuana cops finding me, that was just bad luck."

Esteban says, "No, they were tipped."

Hubbell looks at him in disbelief.

"You're wrong."

"I'm not wrong," Esteban says, obviously annoyed. "My Captain talked the the Chief of Police in Tijuana. Some guy ratted you out."

"Tompkins?"

"I don't know. They said the guy was very soft spoken, like he was trying to disguise his voice and he used precise English almost like a college professor."

I must have reacted noticeably because Aaron turns to me and says, "What?"

"The guy who spilled the story to the L.A.Times. Lou Cioffi says the guy was soft spoken, educated and used a lot of big words and that is definitely not Tompkins." I look at Hubbell. "Sound like anybody you know?" I ask. He shakes his head. "Maybe someone you recently met at the Naked Apollo."

He shakes his head."I didn't meet anybody at the Apollo, not anyone I'd spend time with."

"Who'd you call, Mr. Cox?"

Aaron Kleinschmidt, career cop, is now leaning forward across the table and fixing a cold stare into Cox's eyes. He repeats himself calmly but firmly. "Who did you call?"

Hubbell is starting to sweat. "No, I----"

"The Tijuana cops followed you to Ensenada. They were on the pier because someone told them that's where you'd be. They didn't follow you there because they would have grabbed you immediately. No, it was a phone tip and it came from someone you talked to. Someone you told that you would be on that pier and that you were being picked up by U.S. cops. Now, who, Mr. Cox, and if you tell me 'I don't know" I'm going to send half your teeth into your gut."

Hubbell shakes his head. "No, he wouldn't," he says.

"Who's he?" I ask.

"He wouldn't have done it. He loves me."

"Who are we talking about here, Mr. Cox?" Aaron asks.

"Boyd Larrabee. But he's back at the ranch in San Antonio."

"And who the hell is this Boyd Larrabee?" Aaron wants to know.

"The ranch's bookkeeper," I say.

"And you two are friends?" Aaron says. "Very good friends?"

Hubbell glares at him. "Very good friends, Sergeant," he says with hard emphasis on the 'very'.

"And you called him from Ensenada?" I ask

"Just to tell him I was okay and to let him know about the plan to get me back into the States."

Aaron nods. "And this Larrabee guy, he works for Tompkins."

"Of course."

"And Tompkins signs his paychecks?"

"Yes, but---"

"And how long after he was hired did this guy start making advances toward you?"

Hubbell squints.

"No, you're wrong. It wasn't like that. He---" He stops.

"He what?"

Cox looks away. "What are you saying?"

"You know what I'm saying," Aaron says.

Cox slumps back in his chair and stares unseeing at his half-finished plate of eggs.

"But he loves me," he says.

"I'm sure he does," Aaron says quietly as he backs off and resumes eating his breakfast.

CHAPTER EIGHTEEN

It takes nearly an hour for Aaron and me to drive to police headquarters at 150 North Los Angeles Street where Lieutenant Overton maintains his office. It's a few minutes past eight o'clock when he meets us there and we deliver Hubbell Cox into his custody. Cox affirms that he has accompanied us voluntarily which means basically that our foray into Mexico was nothing more than doing a favor for a friend who needed a ride home. The fact that a Tijuana policeman was shot in the knee is swept under the rug and it is unlikely that either he or his pals will broach the subject in public. The federales, the Mexican national police, take a dim view of local law enforcement officials who steal money from visiting Americanos unless, of course, they have a piece of the action. In this case I think the three rogue cops were acting very much on their own and silence is their best defense against instant termination.

Hubbell is told that he will be booked as a material witness and kept isolated for his own protection. He says he understands. It is becoming clear to him that Elvira and Willie Babbitt did not have his best interest at heart when they helped him "escape" to Mexico.

Having nothing left to do, Aaron and I head for the parking

lot where Bunny's battered Plymouth has been sitting since yesterday afternoon. Aaron congratulates me on not screwing up which I take as high praise, given the faint smile on his lips and a twinkle in his eye. We are not yet blood brothers but I think this shared adventure has brought us closer together. Not that he would ever admit it.

As I head over the hill toward Van Nuys and the comfort of my little house, I can feel the adrenalin draining from my body. I am grateful it's a Saturday and the office does not beckon. Twice my eyes start to close and I have to snap my head up to avoid swerving into the wrong lane. By the time I get inside my bedroom I am in a complete state of collapse and I throw myself onto the bed. Sleep washes over me in a matter of minutes.

My sleep was obviously deep because I remember nothing until I am awakened by the insistent rudeness of my telephone. I glance at the clock on my bedside table. It reads 5:12. I have been out for over eight hours. I sit up, trying to clear my head as the phone continues to ring. Whoever is on the other end of the line is not giving up. I get to my feet and make my way into the kitchen where my one and only phone hangs from the wall.

"Hello," I say.

"Mr. Bernardi?"

"Yeah. Who's this?"

"Roy Fitzgerald. We met last Tuesday at the Naked Apollo. You gave me your card."

"Oh, sure," I say as my head starts to clear.

"You asked me to call you if your friend showed up. Well, he's here."

"No, he isn't," I say. "I mean, he's at police headquarters. Locked up."

"Afraid not. He walked in here about twenty minutes ago

and from what I can see, he looks scared to death. I think he's being chased."

"Put him on the phone," I say.

"Don't think I can. He's in a room in the back near the kitchen and he's not coming out."

I think about that for a couple of moments and then I say, "Okay, I'm on my way. Can you hold him there?"

"I can try," Fitzgerald says.

I hang up and take the car keys from the counter and start for the door. I hesitate, then move quickly back into the bedroom and grab my .25 Beretta from a bedside drawer. I don't know what's going on but something tells me I will be better off with something in my trouser pocket besides lint.

Thirty minutes later I turn off Highland Avenue onto the little side street on which Naked Apollo is located. Unlike the last time I was here there are cars everywhere. I shouldn't be surprised. It's six o'clock on a Saturday. Party time. Before I can get discouraged, I get lucky. A car is just pulling out from a curbside space three doors down from the front entrance. As he leaves I glide in to replace him. I get out of the car and start toward the entrance and that's when I notice the late model Olds parked across the street. Willie Babbitt is behind the wheel. Little Bob Brown is in the passenger seat beside him. They are both staring at me as I approach the door to the club. I give them a smiling salute. They don't respond. Something ugly is coming down here. I pat my trouser leg and feel comforted. Yeah, my pistol is still there and it's loaded. At least I think it's loaded. Maybe I should have checked.

Roy Fitzgerald is sitting at the bar occupying the same spot as the last time I saw him. I move in behind him and tap him on the shoulder. He swivels around to face me.

"Is he still here?" I ask.

Roy nods. "I told him you were on the way. He seemed very relieved."

"Thanks for calling."

"De nada," he says. "Did you notice the big guy across the street at the wheel of the Olds?"

"I did."

"He's your friend's trouble."

"I know."

"He walked in here about fifteen minutes ago, him and the little shrimp with him. He was looking all around, searching for your buddy. When he started for the back room I got up and braced him."

"Took guts," I say. "He's a big boy."

"So am I," Roy grins, "I very loudly told him to get the hell out of here. That's the key. Loudly. Make sure everybody hears. My friends and I don't like strangers coming in here much. If they're not cops, they're usually queer bashers. Either way we don't want them around. So when the guys all started to press in on them and Bruce came out from behind the bar carrying his ax handle, they decided to leave."

"And now they're sitting out there, waiting."

Roy nods. "Let 'em wait," he says.

I walk back toward the kitchen. On my left is a door marked 'Private'. I try the handle. It's locked. I knock softly. No response. I knock louder. "Hubbell, it's Joe Bernardi," I say. Again quiet but then I hear a stirring and the sound of a bolt being thrown. The door opens a crack. Hubbell peers out. There are deep circles under his bloodshot eyes and his skin is pale. He has the haunted look of a man on the run for his life.

"I'm alone," I say.

He opens the door a little wider and I quickly slip in the opening. He closes it and slides the bolt.

"What the hell happened? You're supposed to be in custody," I say.

He grabs a half-full water bottle from a table and drinks deep. Then he looks at me. "Boyd," he says. "No, maybe not Boyd. I don't know. They used his name."

"Who's we? What's going on?"

He sits down, shaking his head. "It was at least an hour ago, probably more like two. The guard comes to my cell and tells me my lawyer is here. I tell him I don't have a lawyer. He tells me the guy is waiting for me out by the booking room. He's arranged for my release. The guard tells me the lawyer was hired by a guy named Larrabee. I perk up. I thought Boyd had abandoned me so I hurry out. The lawyer's taken care of all the paperwork. He says Boyd is waiting for me in his car outside. But when I walk out the main entrance I don't see Boyd, I see Willie and Elvira standing by a car across the street and for a moment I freeze. Then I realize I can't let them get their hands on me and I see a yellow cab up near the corner and I start to run for it. Willie starts chasing after me but I'm not worried because Willie may be big but he's also clumsy and slow. I hop in the cab and we take off and when I look back I see Willie running back toward his car. I have the cabbie bring me here because it's the safest place I know but of course, I was stupid. It didn't take Willie long to find the cab driver who told him where I'd been dropped off." He looks up at me fearfully. "Are they still outside?"

I nod.

"Maybe you should have turned around and gone back into police headquarters," I say

Hubbell shakes his head. "I think not. You have no idea how

powerful old man Tompkins is, He bribes, he threatens, he gets what he wants. They would have gotten to me even in a guarded cell in police headquarters."

"Not here in California," I say.

"Anywhere," Hubbell responds.

"And what makes you so sure Tompkins is involved in all this?"

"Willie," Hubbell says. "Willie won't take a dump unless the old man says it's okay."

"You sure about that?" I ask.

"Willie's been doing the old man's dirty work for twenty-one years, ever since he got out of prison. Jed was the only one who'd hire him. Willie doesn't forget things like that. Believe it or not, there's a real person underneath all that muscle."

"And if Jed Tompkins ordered Willie to kill his son-in-law?"

"Then Bryce'd be dead. But he didn't. Jed doesn't work that way. To Jed, death is quick and easy. He has his own methods. They take a lot longer and they're a lot more painful."

"You, know somebody is damned anxious to pin this murder on you," I say.

He nods. "That they are."

"And you can't stay here forever," I say.

Hubbell nods helplessly.

"I know a place they'll never find you," I say. "Hold tight. I have to talk to Fitzgerald. Lock the door behind me,"

I throw the bolt and open the door and step out into the corridor. I hear the door close behind me and the bolt being secured and then I go in search of Roy Fitzgerald. I hope he's still here.

He is and when I tell him my plan, he readily agrees. I go back to the room to get Hubbell while Roy goes to the bar to enlist the aid of Bruce the bartender.

At first Hubbell is hesitant but when I explain to him that my phone is unlisted as is my address and that the studio never ever under any circumstances gives out personal information to outsiders about its employees, he reluctantly agrees to go along with my plan.

A few minutes later we are looking out the front window of the club onto the narrow side street. A four year old Dodge sedan approaches with Roy Fitzgerald at the wheel. He double parks next to Willie's Olds, hemming him in so close that he can't open his driver's side door. At the same time, Bruce steps out the front door onto the sidewalk. He's carrying the ax handle and slapping it into his left hand, all the while keeping his gaze fixated on Wiliie and Little Bob. This is our cue. We start out the door surrounded by four of the club's taller patrons and we move as a unit along the sidewalk toward the Plymouth. Bruce moves with us but his eyes never leave Willie who is trapped immobile behind the steering wheel of the Olds. Once at the Plymouth, I slip behind the wheel and Hubbell gets in the passenger seat. A moment later we pull out into the street and head toward La Brea a couple of blocks away. I feel Willie's eyes boring into me and as we pass him by, I give him a smile and a cheery wave. He doesn't return it.

I am so full of myself and so proud of my victory that I fail to notice the grey Ford coupe that pulls into traffic behind us and follows us over the hill and into the San Fernando Valley.

CHAPTER NINETEEN

I pull into the empty garage, then lower the door to keep the Plymouth invisible to prying eyes. It's an overabundance of caution but at the moment, I have no reason to trust anyone except maybe ever-faithful Glenda Mae. Hubbell and I enter the kitchen thorough the side door. He asks directions to the bathroom and I head for the phone to call Lt. Overton. I get the desk sergeant instead.

"Well, where is he?" I ask. "How can I get in touch with him?"

"II's Sunday, sir. I expect he's home with his family."

"Can you give me that number?"

"No, sir, I cannot," the sergeant says.

"Look, Sergeant, this is urgent. Will you please call the lieutenant immediately and tell him to phone me right away. My name is Joe Bernardi. He'll know what it's about." I give the sergeant my phone number and hang up just as Hubbell is coming back into the kitchen. Then I do something I should have done long ago. I take the Beretta out of my pocket and check the clip. It's full and I replace it, then pull the slide and chamber a round.

"What's that for?" Hubbell asks cautiously, eyeing my weapon.

"Target practice," I say, "just in case one of the targets tries to break into the house."

"You said we'd be safe here," Hubbell says.

"And we will be provided the grey Ford I kept seeing in my rearview mirror the past few miles wasn't actually following us." I see his look and I've scared the piss out of him. "Relax, Hubbell. I'm paranoid. Nobody followed us. You want something to eat?"

He shakes his head and goes out of the kitchen into the living room where he opens the venetian blinds and looks out into the street. He reacts sharply and I move in next to him. You've probably heard that old chestnut which goes, even if you're paranoid, it doesn't mean people aren't out to get you. Across the street, sitting quietly, engine off, is the grey Ford I'd spotted earlier. I was wrong. We were followed. There's a man sitting behind the wheel but a shadow across his face masks his features.

"It's Boyd," Hubbell says.

"You don't know that."

"It's him. I know it is," Hubbell says starting for the front door. I get there first, blocking his way.

"Don't be a fool. Even if it is, he's not your friend. He's working with Willie."

"No," he says adamantly.

"Yes!" I shout as if talking to a petulant child. I slip the deadbolt on the door and point. "Get in the kitchen." When he doesn't move, I shove him. "Get in the kitchen, god damn it!" I do everything but pull the gun on him and he backs off, then turns in a huff and strides back into the kitchen. I follow him.

"Five'll get you ten, your pal Boyd is the one who called Lou Cioffi at the Times and gave him the facts about Bryce's death, making sure the homosexual angle got publicized and that the finger of suspicion pointed squarely at you."

"No,----"

"And ten'll get you twenty that he's the one who tipped the Tijuana police that you were coming across the border with a satchel full of cash and don't tell me no because Willie Babbitt is in this thing up to his adam's apple and where Willie's involved, J. Farrell Tompkins is involved and J. Farrell Tompkins is the guy who hired your boyfriend to keep close to you and report back to him. Do you get it, Hubbell? You're a patsy and if you don't want to fry in the San Quentin hot seat, you'd better wise up starting now."

He says nothing because he has nothing to say. Life's a bitch when you finally realize your love has been betrayed and that's where Hubbell Cox now finds himself.

"I have a call in to Lt. Overton. When he calls back I'll have him dispatch a metro cruiser to roust the grey Ford and if it is your pal Boyd, take him in for intensive questioning." I check my watch. "Matter of fact I should have heard from Overton by now. Maybe that desk sergeant needs a little goosing."

I go to the phone and lift the receiver. I dial the first three numbers and aside from a vicious slam to the back of my head that's all I remember as I slide to the floor and everything goes black.

I'm not out for long. My head starts to function long before the message reaches my arms and legs. Up, boy. Move. Get to your feet. I think it but I can't quite do it. Then slowly I feel movement in my fingers and toes and I am able to grab onto a kitchen chair and pull myself up into a sitting position. I spot the heavy crystal vase on the floor beside me. It hasn't come within sniffing distance of a flower since the day Bunny left and still I have kept it on the kitchen table, God knows why.

I look at my watch. Only four minutes have passed since

I started to make the phone call. With my head feeling like a pinata on the fifth of May, I get to my feet and stumble into the living room. I throw up the venetian blinds. The grey Ford is gone and so is Hubbell. I turn and fumble my way back into the kitchen where I grab the phone and call headquarters. I reach the same desk sergeant who tells me that Lt. Overton is not answering his phone and is likely out for the day. He asks if he should keep trying and I tell him no. I'm not going to be much help to Hubbell sitting around my kitchen. The problem is, where do I go and what do I do?

One thing is certain. Hubbell Cox is in desperate trouble. The plan to have him cross the border into Mexico and then be killed as a fleeing fugitive has failed. But they still need him as the fall guy. They can't just kill him and dump him. That would raise more questions than it would answer. They can't kill him and bury the body for the same reason. Loose ends attract nosy reporters. Twenty one years ago a New York City judge named Crater disappeared and people are still looking for him. So much for that scenario. And then my mind gloms onto a third possibility which is right out of a B movie, the phony suicide with the even phonier confession note. Is it possible? Sure. Is it probable? I don't know but it sure solves a lot of problems for some very bad people. And if there's to be a suicide, where? In a sealed garage inside a car with the motor running? Hara kiri in front of a living room fireplace? A bullet to the brain seated at a desk in the den? Or maybe propped up in bed with an empty water glass and an emptier bottle of pills near at hand. All of these possibilities suggest one thing. Home. And home at the moment for Hubbell Cox is a Malibu beach house owned by a person unknown presently cavorting on the sands of a St. Tropez beach.

I know someone who probably could give me that address

but I can't call her because the owner of the guest house where she is staying is a stewardess with Pan Am whose name I do not kmow and whose phone number I do not have. Okay, but I do have an address. I pick up my car keys. I check to make sure I have my wallet. I pat my trouser pocket. Uh,oh. Empty. The son of a bitch has stolen my gun. Well, for his sake, I hope he knows how to use it.

It's past seven thirty but it's also May going on June and it's still light out. By eight thirty the sky to the west will be turning blue and salmon pink and by nine darkness will settle in. But for now I can see where I'm going and when I turn off Laurel Canyon onto the side street, I see the little cottage ahead. I pull into the driveway and park behind a Lincoln Cosmopolitan which I find odd because it doesn't seem Jenny's kind of car. Maybe the stew is back from Rome.

I ring the doorbell and wait but no one comes to the door. I push the bell again, more insistently. Nothng. Maybe she's nap-pjng. If so she'll have to get up. I desperately need that address. I try knocking and succeed in skinning my knuckles. If it weren't for the Lincoln I could assume that she was out but I know she's not. For a moment I stand there frustrated and consider tossing a brick through the window but then settle for the Cosmopolitan's horn. I open the car door and lean on it and it's loud enough to be mistaken for an A-Bomb alert. If that doesn't catch her atten-tion I'm pretty sure it wlll arouse the neighbors and instigate a call to the cops.

The front door opens and she appears. Her hair is tousled and she's wearing a man's white shirt and nothing else that I can see. I stride to the door and brush past her into the cottage.

"I need help," I say.

"You sure do," she says icily, shutting the door.

At that moment, the door to the bedroom opens and J. Farrell Tompkins emerges. He's wearing an undershirt and a pair of slacks and his feet are bare. Maybe he's been giving himself a pedicure.

I look from Tompkins back to Jenny

"Sorry," I say.

"No need, young fella," Tompkins says. "The lady and I have all night."

Jenny glowers ar me.

"What are you doing here, Joe?"

"Trying to save somebody's life," I say. "I'm hoping you'll help me. If not I'll assume you're part of the problem."

Tompkins tosses me a good-old-boy smile. "Now, Joe, no need to say something like that."

I turn and glare at him. "I think there is, Jed. One man is dead, probably on your orders. Another man's about to die to protect your worthless hide. You may even come after me. I'm being pretty troublesome and it's my guess that when you run up against a pesky fly, you swat it. Is that how it works, Jed?"

"You need a drink, son," Tompkins says.

"No, what I need is an address." I look over at Jenny. "Where is Hubbell Cox staying in Malibu?"

"I don't know," she says.

"Bullshit."

"I have a phone number, that's all. Do you want it?"

"You mean, do I want to call the number and let everyone know I'm on the way? I don't think so." I take a couple of angry steps toward her. "I need the damned address before somebody kills him!"

"I don't have it!" she shouts back. She hesitates, thoughtfully. "He said he was living next door to a writer. An old guy. Been around for years."

"What's his name?"

"I'm trying to remember. Hannibal. Something like that. Hannibal. Hanniford."

It comes to me. "Haviland?"

"Haviland. Yes, that's it," she says.

"Where's your phone book", I say.

She points to a table on which the phone sits. "Middle drawer," she says.

I yank open the drawer and take out the phone directory. Quickly I scan the H's and I find it.

"He's in the Colony, on the water."

I tear the page from the book and hurry to the door.

"Bernardi!"

I turn as Tompkins calls my name.

The old man glares at me with genuine rage written all over his face. "I don't give a damn what you think of me but hear this good, boy. I told you once and I'm telling you again. I did not kill Bryce and I didn't order anybody to do it for me. As God is my witness, that is the truth. Believe it or not, as you wish."

He turns and goes back into the bedroom and shuts the door. I look over at Jenny.

"You got everything you need?" she asks coldly.

"I do," I say. "How about you?" It's a cheap shot and as soon as I say it, I regret it.

Jenny reddens and looks away.

"That was crude. Sorry," I say.

She looks back at me. "No need. A girl's got to make her way in the world."

"Yeah, I guess she does," I say. I go to the front door and open it. "Good luck, Jenny," I say and then I'm out the door.

When I slip behind the wheel of the Plymouth, I see her

standing in the doorway watching me leave. There's a look of sadness in her eyes and I feel sorry for her. She's operating like a high priced hooker and she doesn't need to. She's too bright for that but maybe she doesn't know it. Too bad. We had a few laughs together but boiled down to essentials, I was a potential stepping stone and not much more. I decide to file this one away in a place where I won't forget it.

CHAPTER TWENTY

Because it's still light out, I'm able to barrel down Laurel Canyon toward the Valley side, risking life and limb because I am pretty sure time is running out for Hubbell Cox. The good news is, I know where I'm going. The Malibu Colony is an upscale beach front community for film artists most of whom are obscenely well off and a few who got in before the prices soared skyward. I suspect that Joshua Haviland fits the latter category. I don't know him personally but I do know he's a respected old timer who started out writing dialogue cards for the silents and graduated to scripts when sound came in. I know he works a lot for Paramount and was once nominated for an Oscar.

When I hit Ventura Boulevard I head west and look for a phone booth. I spot one at the edge of a Texaco station and pull up next to it. I get that same desk sergeant but this time he has better news. Lt. Overton wants to speak with me first chance I get. The sergeant gives me Overton's number but I tell him I'm out of change and I give him the number of the phone booth. Two minutes later, Overton calls me.

"What happened?" he asks.

I tell him.

"Son of a bitch," he says.

"My thoughts exactly," I say.

"They could have taken him anywhere," Overton says.

"No, I think they took him to the beach house in Malibu."

I explain about the loan of the beach house to Hubbell by his friend and give him Josh Haviland's address next door.

"Okay, I'm on my way. I'll call ahead and have a cruiser from the Sheriff's department check it out."

"I'll meet you there," I say.

"No, you won't," Overton says sharply. "You're a civilian. Stay put."

"Hell, no," I say. "I risked my neck getting this guy out of Mexico. I'll be there in twenty minutes. Try not to shoot me."

I hang up and get back in my car and continue down Ventura and then slide onto the 101 at the Woodland Hills on ramp. At Las Virgenes Road I turn off and follow the winding mountain road down toward the Pacific Coast Highway which parallels the ocean. The light is fading quickly now and because there are no street lamps, I have my high beams on. Even so I am forced to slow down to no more than 25. As I press forward I wonder if I am on a fool's errand. I may be totally wrong and if so, I am going to look like a jerk in Lt. Overton's eyes. I ignore the fact that I may already have attained that distinction.

I go over it again in my head and there are two things that I know for sure. Willie Babbitt is at the center of things and Hubbell's boy pal, Boyd Larabee, is hooked in with Willie. Back at the Naked Apollo, Roy Fitzgerald had hemmed Willie in so he couldn't follow but Larrabee must have been parked up the street and got on my tail when Willie couldn't. As to things that don't fit, the lawyer is the big one. To hear Hubbell tell it this was no dime store shyster. He was well dressed, well spoken and self-assured.

He also had all the right paperwork and he didn't take any crap from the cops on duty because they apparently let him go without a whimper. It doesn't add up. What's a guy like that doing working for Willie Babbitt? Answer? He isn't. And that means he was hired by someone with a patina of class. If I believe Jed Tompkins, and I'm starting to, that leaves me with two possibilities: the not so grieving widow or Hubbell's duplicitous boyfriend. My head starts to throb. I need aspirin desperately.

At the end of Las Virgenes I take a left turn onto the Pacific Coast Highway and head south. It's totally dark now but there are street lamps lining PCH. After a few hundred yards I pass the sign that says "Entering Malibu" and a short distance later, I turn onto Old Malibu Road and start to drive slowly toward the ocean and the beach front properties. I keep my eye out for Overton or the Sheriff's cruiser but I don't spot either. I pull to the side of the road. It occurs to me that driving up and parking in front of the beach house might not be a really smart move. I get out of the car and start to walk. I pat my trouser pocket where my Beretta used to be. I feel very vulnerable without it.

I check a street sign and continue walking. I'm in the right place. Three doors up I see the name on the mailbox. J. Haviland. I'm standing in front of his south side neighbor. The house is dark and shuttered. The lawn is unkempt. There is a "For Sale" sign planted in the front yard. I continue on. There's apparently no one home at Haviland's but at the next house I can make out a dim light coming through the cracks of the drawn shades,

I peer at my watch but in the darkness it's hard to read. I think it says nine-twenty but in any case, Overton should have been here by now and so should those Sheriff's deputies. I'm pretty sure I should stay put until help arrives but I feel foolish standing alone in the dark. What the hell, it won't hurt to make a cautious reconnaissance. I move forward and start down the path that separates the beach house from Haviland's place next door. It is very quiet. I hear the lapping of the tide against the beach and the far off sounds of warning buoys and the occasional baying of a dog, but from the house, I hear nothing. That same crescent moon that was following us last night in Mexican waters is with us again and I am having trouble keeping my footing on the rutted dirt pathway that leads to the rear of the house. I start to pass by a window where the shade is slightly askew. I stand on tiptoe and stare inside. It is some kind of small office or den with a desk and a couple of chairs. A lamp on the desk has been turned on but there is no other illumination. And then I look down and see the body of a man lying in the shadows. It's partially hidden by the desk and it isn't moving and I know that whoever it is, he is dead.

I hurry to the rear of the house and step up onto the porch. I test the handle to the rear door and it turns easily. Cautiously I push the door open and pause to listen. I hear nothing. I step inside and find myself at one end of a hallway that traverses the length of the house to the front door. I move forward. Ahead on my left is an open doorway. This is the same room I just peered into. I step inside and look toward the desk. I get a clearer look at the body now and it's too small to be Hubbell Cox. I move in closer. Boyd Larrabee's eyes are staring sightlessly at the ceiling and there is a bloody bullet hole in his forehead. I touch his hand. He is dead but his body is still warm. I back up and edge out of the room.

There's another room ahead on the right and a light glows from under the door. I'm not sure I want to see what's in there but I know I have to. I turn the door handle and look inside. Hubbell Cox is lying on the bed, very still. Blood is oozing from a wound in his right temple and there's a pistol in his hand. When I get closer I see that it's my Beretta automatic. Next to his hand is a single sheet of paper with a message. I know enough not to touch it but I crane my neck so I can read what it says. "Bryce tried to destroy us. I destroyed him first. Now Boyd and I will be at peace where no one can torment us." It is written in block letters and unsigned. It could have been written by the meter reader. The cops will buy it because it's neat and convenient and gets the newspapers off their backs. And I suspect Overton will keep his mouth shut no matter what he might believe privately. The LAPD is like every other beauracracy. To get along, go along. Lieutenants don't get to be lieutenants by fighting the system.

Just then I hear a sudden rush of water. Someone has flushed a toilet. I jump back from the bed frantically. I need to get out of there. I hurry to the window. It's unlatched and I try to raise it. It gives easily for about ten inches and then jams. I tug harder but to no avail. I hear movement out in in the hallway. Somebody is approaching. No way can I squeeze through the tiny opening. I look around frantically and spot the closet. The door is accordion-like with horizontal slats and I duck inside and pull it shut. Through the slats I get a clear view of the room and I manage to stifle a gasp when Willie steps through the doorway. He is holding a handkerchief in his right hand and he approaches the bed. He leans in and takes another look at Hubbell's dead body. Then he starts to wipe the bedside table and the lamp clean of any possible fingerprints. He looks around the room for a final check and his gaze falls on the partially open window. He steps toward it, puzzled, and his brain tries to put it together. He turns back into the room and stands very still. I hold my breath. Its only for a few seconds but it seems like minutes and then he casts his eyes toward the closet. He slips his hand under his jacket and pulls out a .45 automatic. As he does he starts toward the closet door. Instinctively I back up. If I can look out, it's very possible he can look in.

I start to shudder. I am only moments away from being blown in half by a homicidal cretin. I know only one thing. I cannot just stand here like a cigar store Indian and let him shoot me uncontested. I ease back slowly inching my way into the hanging clothing behind me. I have one chance. I need that one second where he doesn't automatically see me. Willie pushes at the door and it spreads open. I am staring into his face but if he sees me, he gives no sign. I leap forward and throw a balled fist at his face and I hear a crunch. It's his jaw or my hand but either way, he grunts and falls backward onto the floor. In that instant I dash past him, out the bedroom door and race toward the rear of the house. I fling open the rear door, two quick steps on the porch and I leap onto the sand and start to run. The sand is thick and I fall. I struggle to my feet and again try to run but I feel like I'm slogging in tar.

I hear the door slam and look behind me. Willie is in pursuit with his gun in his right hand. It's dark. I'm probably not a good target and I'm pretty sure he doesn't want to risk a shot and wake the neighbors. Still, he can't allow me to escape. He'll do what he has to do.

I look behind me. He's closing in. Because I'm not looking ahead I suddenly stumble over something in the sand, twisting my ankle and going down in pain. It's a child's pail and shovel. I try to stand. The pain shoots up my leg as I limp forward. Just then I hear two quick shots and a cry of pain. I turn and see Willie standing motionless. He turns and looks behind him. Two more shots ring out and Willie shudders and then falls in a heap onto the sand. Farther back, coming from the beach house I see a man running toward us. When he gets close, I recognize Lt. Overton, gun in hand. He stops when he reaches Willie, keeping the gun trained on Willie's motionless body. With his foot, he rolls Willie over and sees that he is dead. He looks over at me.

"Are you all right?" he asks.

I tell him I am.

"You are one dumb son of a bitch," he says. "Dumb but lucky."

I'm in no mood to argue.

CHAPTER TWENTY ONE

t is ten minutes to midnight and still Sunday evening and we are all jammed into the Malibu-Lost Hills Sheriff's station which seems busier than Gilhooley's bar on St. Patrick's Day. The Sheriff's Department in the person of Captain Noah Peckinpaugh, the station's commander, has stepped aside and ceded jurisdiction of this case to the LAPD in light of the connection to the murder of Bryce Tremayne and the hand printed confession found next to Hubbell Cox's body. A forensic team from the city is at the beach house taking photos and compiling evidence. An ambulance and a coroner's van are standing by to transport the three bodies to the Los Angeles City Morgue where autopsies will be performed. If the medical examiner comes back with anything but death by gunshot, I will be astonished.

Peckinpaugh greeted me warmly when I arrived. Our history goes back two years when I shot and killed a man in self-defense using the same Beretta which the cops have now confiscated as the weapon used in the deaths of Boyd Larrabee and Hubbell Cox. At the time I had no permit to carry a weapon and we both knew it, but since the "victim" was a worthless psychopath who considered murder an amusing diversion, Peckinpaugh allowed me to fill out the permit application, back dating it several days before the incident. We have been friends ever since.

Both Overton and Peckinpaugh are busy taking statements and filling out paperwork. I've already given my statement but there are things they need to verify which is why I am still sitting here long after I should be home in bed. I have had supper in the form of a Hershey bar and a bag of peanuts from a vending machine. The two cups of coffee were free courtesy of the Sheriff. My adrenalin is wearing off, my ass is beginning to ache from sitting on a hard wooden bench and the only reading matter available is a year old copy of 'Field and Stream'. My interest in fly fishing for small mouthed bass is zero so I try to curl up and close my eyes. The bench fights me every step of the way.

I hear a commotion at the doorway and look up as Little Bob Brown is brought in, flanked by two burly deputies who each have him by an arm. They plop him down on the other end of my bench and admonish him not to move, then walk off to report in. Little Bob and I exchange glances. I nod. He doesn't.

"What are you doing here?" I ask.

He doesn't answer.

"I'm surprised you weren't at the beach house with Willie."

"I don't do murder," he says quietly.

I nod.

"Maybe you were just acting as a lookout."

"I was in that greasy spoon diner across from the pier havin' coffee when the cops came in and grabbed me."

"A.P.B.?" I ask

"I guess so," he says. "I'd been there at least two hours. Ask the fry cook."

"Tell it to Overton. I'm not a cop."

Little Bob falls silent for a moment or two.

"I guess he's dead," he says.

"Willie?"

"Yeah. Willie," he says.

I nod. "He's dead," I say.

Little Bob falls silent again.

"You kill him?" he asks.

I shake my head.

"I told him he'd get himself killed. He wouldn't listen. When it came to her he never listened."

"Her?"

"Elvira."

"What about her?"

"He was in love with her. Dumb bastard,"

"How long had that been going on?"

"Ever since he came to work for Tompkins twenty one years ago. She was like nineteen. Prettiest thing you ever saw. Willie was twenty-somethng. An ex-con. She never looked at him twice."

"Unless she needed something from him."

"That's right," Little Bob says. "Then she's all over him, makin' big eyes and cooin' at him. Like I said, dumb bastard."

"And then one day she wants Bryce dead."

He nods. "She'd had enough. That last punch to the face, that was the one that did it. After that Bryce was a dead man."

"So Willie didn't do it on his own?"

"Willie never did anything on his own. She told him to do it. She asked nicely but it was an order and they both knew it. She's the one who figured out how to frame Cox and she's the one who lifted the matchbook from his suit pocket. She told Willie how to stage it and he did it right. Willie wasn't stupid. Maybe he didn't think much on his own but you give him somethin' to do and he does it right. No mistakes."

"Do you have any corroboration? I mean, someone else who can back up your story?"

He glares at me. "I know what corroboration means, mister. I ain't no dummy."

"Then you know that Elvira is just as guilty of murder as Willie."

"Is she?" A wry smile crosses his lips.

"Under the law---"

"Screw the law," he says. "You don't seriously think that J. Farrell Tompkins' daughter is gonna be arrested and tried for murder."

"When you tell the lieutenant----"

"I ain't tellin' the lieutenant anything," he says. "I got a good job with Tompkins. Decent pay, three squares a day. I can't complain."

"You mean that, don't you?"

"Hell, yes, I mean it," Little Bob says in annoyance. "People get themselves killed all the time. Some deserve it, most don't. Those who deserve it, I say God is guidin' somebody's hand and to hell with them."

Now it's my turn to fall silent. Finally I say, "You know, I feel an obligation to tell all this is Lt. Overton."

Little Bob smiles. "Do you?"

"Yes, I do."

"Well, you go ahead then," he says. "Course, I'll call you a liar and you got nothin' else so you'll be just be makin' a fool of yourself, but if that's what you want to do, you do it."

I shrug. "Conscience demands it," I say.

"Kinda fancy, the way you put things."

"Writer's disease. Incurable."

"Well, like I said, you go on if you don't mind bein' laughed at. I'll tell you who won't be laughin'. The old man. He'll be madder'n hell. He'll never let you know it but he'll start takin' you down bit by bit and a year or two from now when your life has turned to crap, you might even look back and figure out why." He smiles. "Like I say, up to you."

"Bernardi!"

I look up. A Sheriff's deputy is standing in the doorway to Peckinpaugh's office and waving to me. "The lieutenant wants to see you."

I get up and start to cross the squad room. I look back. Little Bob is staring after me, still smiling.

When I go into the office, Overton hands me two sheets of paper stapled together. "Your statement," he says. "Read it over and if it's accurate, sign it and we'll get you out of here."

I nod and quickly scan it.

"Looks okay to me," I say.

"Anything you want to add?" Overton asks.

I look up at him, then over to Peckinpaugh. I wonder what they know and if this is some kind of test. I think about Little Bob's warning. I'm not afraid of Tompkins though I probably should be. But he's right about one thing. With Willie dead, there's no proof of anything. Elvira's untouchable and all I can do is make a fool of myself. No, I've had enough of this case and these people. I just want out.

"Looks okay to me," I say. I place it on the desk and sign and date it and hand it back to Overton.

Peckinpaugh comes around his desk and takes me by the arm and leads me out the door. "You take care of yourself now, Joe. Go home and get some shuteye."

"I will."

He signals to the deputy. "Hank, drive Mr. Bernardi back to the Colony so he can pick up his car."

"Will do, Captain. Right this way, sir," he says to me and we head for the entrance. I give Little Bob one last look but by now he's engrossed in 'Field and Stream'.

Hank's an easy going, gregarious kind of guy who likes to chat. He's been a deputy for six years, loves his job, loves Malibu and most of all loves his wife and his four year old son. He did his time in the Pacific theater and would have been on a Honshu beach if Truman hadn't dropped the bomb. He thinks he has a lot to be grateful for and thanks God for it every day. He mentions the Diety in passing and doesn't dwell on Him. To my mind Hank is a meat and potatoes kind of guy and he and those like him are the backbone of this country. Hardworking, down to earth and unpretentious, he's a far cry from the many self centered narcissists I have to deal with in my day to day life.

"Too bad you guys couldn't have gotten there a little sooner," I say. "Might have saved some lives."

"Maybe so," he grunts, "but probably not. We had our hands full with the rumble in the Zuma Beach parking lot."

I look at him disbelievingly. "You're kidding. A rumble in Malibu?"

He nods. "City kids from East L.A. White gangs, Mex gangs, Negro gangs. They're all the same. Looking for somebody to fight. Too many innocents getting hurt back in the city so the cops started busting heads. These kids got tired of going to the hospital so they started coming up here where nobody'd bother them. Figured maybe that me and my boys were soft. We showed 'em tonight they were wrong about that."

I shake my head. "First I've heard of it."

"Oh, yeah," Hank says. "Must have been about fifty of them showed up just before dark. There were six of us. Three squad cars. We tried talking nice and when that didn't work we went after them with our batons. By then it was dark and they scattered. Got away, all but two of them. We put the fear of God into those two, told 'em if they showed up again, they'd be lookin' at more than just batons. They got the message. Anyway, thats when we got the call about the beach house in the Colony and by the time we showed up you and that Lieutenant had things pretty much in hand."

"Not me," I say. "I was just a bystander." I point. "That's my car over there. The Plymouth."

He pulls alongside it and I get out.

"Thanks for the ride," I say.

"My pleasure," Hank says. "Drive safe." He pulls away.

I do as I'm told and by one o'clock I turn into my driveway and park the car. I'm about to walk in through the kitchen door when I realize it's been two days since I've collected the mail. I go out to the street and retrieve the contents of my mailbox. There are six or seven letters, mostly bills, I'm sure, and the current issue of The Atlantic Monthly. I bring it all inside and plop it down on the kitchen table while I pour myself a glass of water. As I start to drink I start leafing through the mail and then stop short when I see it. A letter from Bunny. What the hell is this all about, I think. We've never written letters to one another, we've always used the phone.

I sit down at the table and rip open the envelope. It's not a Dear John letter but it's close enough. She is terribly sorry but she won't be able to fly to L.A. for her scheduled visit two weeks hence. Walt has come up with a sensational idea, an entire issue devoted to the Cold War. It'll be called "A Preview of the War We Do Not Want" and it will postulate about a hypothetical war between the United States and the USSR. Bunny's assignment is to spend the next two months traveling across the country and interviewing people from all walks of life to get their views on the tension between the two countries and how it affects their everyday lives. She says she is devastated she won't be seeing me. She'll try to call some time next week.

I stare at the letter for the longest time and then slowly I crumple it up into a ball and toss it into the trash basket. I flip off the light and make my way to the bedroom where I will try to get some sleep.

CHAPTER TWENTY TWO

Monday morning and I'm in the office by nine o'clock and back to my usual routine. A cynic would use the word "rut". I choose not to. I'm delighted to see Glenda Mae, a dependable symbol of sanity in a world gone mad. Murder and near death are behind me. I look forward to days of humdrum predictability. Glenda Mae has no idea what my weekend was like and I am not going to tell her. Or Charlie either. Or Jack Warner, for that matter. Done is done.

The morning Times and the trades are lined up on my desk and Glenda Mae brings me coffee which I sip as I scan the Times. There is nothing in print about the Malibu fiasco because late last night Lou Cioffi hadn't yet gotten wind of it and even if he had, it was probably too late to make the morning edition. I'm sure that tomorrow he'll have plenty to write about but I'll worry about tomorrow tomorrow.

At ten o'clock I go to the screening room for my first look at the rushes for "Streetcar". It's a dynamite scene that occurs just before the end of the film where Stanley, fed up with Blanche and her airs, menaces her and ends up raping her. I am mesmerized. I had heard that Brando was brilliant but my contacts with him had been superficial. He came across as amiable and intelligent and at times a little vague. What I see up on the screen is a genius at work. The pitch perfect inarticulation, the toss of the head, the half-grin, the icy eyes that bettray a smile. It's all Vivien Leigh can do, with her traditional stage training , to keep up with him but somehow she manages it. There is no question, I am watching something very special. Gadge isn't here in the screening room. He watches the rushes very early in the morning before shooting starts. I make a mental note to wander down to the sound stage later and congratulate everyone in sight. This will be a film we can all take pride in.

I head back to my office. The rushes have provided a welcome respite from the irritability I have been feeling ever since I got up this morning. A lot of it has to do with poor dead Hubbell Cox, a sad man who wanted very little from life. Peace and quiet. Love. He had found neither. A vicious newspaperman had shattered his existence with a series of defamatory columns. A self-centered widow with no conscience had tried to destroy what was left by framing him for murder. And now she is back in Texas, safe in the shadow of her powerful father and rid of a husband she had grown to despise. Hollywood dictates retribution for evildoers. Real life demands no such requirement. When it comes to the rich, the privileged and the powerful, justice is nothing more than a seven letter word.

And aside from Elvira Tremayne there are other things that had continued to bother me but now, as certain pieces start to fall into place, anger has replaced bewilderment. Hubbell's death has brought the big picture into focus and suddenly everything is very clear to me. I tell Glenda Mae I am taking the rest of the morning off and I am unreachable. For starters, the cops have my gun and I want it back.

I drive into the lot of police headquarters a few minutes past eleven and start toward the main entrance. As I reach it three men in dress uniform emerge. I recognize the man in the middle. Slim, erect, bespectacled, there is no question it is Chief William Parker. He glances in my direction. I catch his eye. He smiles. I smile back as he passes by. In the past year he's done a praiseworthy job of cleaning up corruption within the ranks of the department. He hasn't gotten them all but it's my feeling he will.

At the main desk on the ground floor, I give my name and ask for Lt. Overton. The sergeant on duty asks me to wait while he checks with Overton's office. After a brief conversation, the sergeant tells me the lieutenant is at the pistol range but should be through in a few minutes. He suggests I take a seat which I do. At eleven twenty-five Overton is striding toward me. We shake hands and he apologizes for keeping me waiting. Not a problem, I say. I had no appointment. He invites me up to his office on the third floor.

"How are you feeling?" he asks after we settle in. He's removed his suit jacket and draped it over the back of his chair and he's hung his pistol and holster on a coat rack by the door. He's also offered coffee which I've refused. I tell him I'm feeling fine, all things considered. He nods in underttanding.

"For us, something like last night is part of the job," Overton says. "It rarely gets that violent or that dangerous but we all know it's part of the package. For a civilian like yourself, I imagine it's a pretty harrowing experience."

"Harrowing. Good word. Terrifying works just as well. "
He smiles.
"So, Joe, what can I do for you?"
"I was wondering when I can expect to get my gun back."
He seems momentariy puzzled. "Your gun. Oh, you mean the Beretta. Sorry, Joe, it may be quite a while. It's part of the evidence."

"Evidence for what? The case is closed. There's not going to be a trial."

"I know, I know," he says defensively, "but it's regulations. Maybe ninety days. I'm not sure. I'd have to check."

"Okay," I say, looking properly disappointed. "Maybe you could call me."

"I can do that," Overton says. "Anything else?"

"No, not really. There is one thing but I hate to bother you with it."

"No bother."

"A friend of mine's writing a script. A police procedural. He had a couple of technical questions I couldn't answer. I told him I'd try to find out how they'd be handled."

"What's his problem?"

"You don't mind?"

"Of course not. Tell me."

"Sure," I say. "Here's the setup. A newspaper reporter. Bad guy. Evil as they come. Say his name is Abe. His wife decides to kill him. We'll call her Abigail. She's got this guy she knows. A big lug, kind of like Moose in "Murder, My Sweet" with Dick Powell."

"Don't know it," Overton says.

"Anyway the lug, whose name is Animal, has been in love with her for years and he'd do anything for her and because he's pretty shady to begin with, killing somebody is no big deal so he agrees. They work out the whole thing so they can frame one of her other friends. He's a pretty decent guy so we'll call him Angel."

Overton smiles. "Very alliterative," he says.

"Right."

"It's also beginning to sound vaguely familiar."

"Hold that thought," I say. "It gets better. So the dirty deed is done, the frame put in place and enter the cop. Every good murder scenario needs a cop."

"Of course," Overton smiles.

"Let's call this one Avaricious."

"That's not really a name," Overton says.

"I know but in this case it fits. Lt. Avaricious starts poking around and the amateur nature of the frame becomes obvious. Now here's where my screenwriter friend gets a little unsure of himself. He doesn't know whether the killer, that is, the wife, contacts the cop or if it's the other way around. Either way the cop gets involved."

"Why?"

"The old reliable, I should imagine. Money. It's a cliche but like all cliches, there a lot of truth to it."

Overton nods.

"So what do you think, Lieutenant?" I ask.

"About what?"

"Does she contact the cop or the other way around?"

He leans back in his swivel chair, smiling and lacing his hands behind his head. "Well, it's not my story but if I were the screenwriter, I'd say the latter."

"The cop contacts her," I say.

"Right."

"Why?"

Overton chuckles. "I don't know. It's not my story."

"Fair enough," I say. "Maybe he's offering professional services. For the sake of argument let's say that this amateurish frame needs a little reworking. For one thing it needs a dead killer. As long as Angel is alive he can proclaim his innocence to high heaven and there's always a chance someone will believe him. But dead, that's something else again, especially if he flees the authorities or even better, leaves behind a remorseful suicide note."

"Absolutely right," Overton says.

"So first things first, the case needs a lot of publicity, especially the seamier elements, so the cop makes an anonymous call to the newspapers and reveals everything about the case. Instant scandal."

Overton shakes his head, "I don't think our police detective would do that," he says.

"I do," I say coldly. "For a huge wad of dough, I think this corrupt son of a bitch would cut his best friend's throat just for the fun of it."

For the first time Overton's eyes narrow in anger but he catches himself almost immediately.

"I think your friend the writer has a real penchant for melodrama," he says.

"Exactly what I told him, but he doesn't listen. Anyway, Angel's in a panic. He has learned that his fingerprints were found at the scene of the murder."

"On a matchbook cover?" Overton asks.

"I don't know but that's an interesting idea. I'll suggest it. In any case, Angel also knows that the police are following him everywhere he goes. He doesn't know where to turn or who to trust but he gets lucky because his good friends, Abigail and Animal, the actual killers, offer to sneak him over the border into Mexico."

"Thoughtful of them," Overton says. He reaches across his desk and takes a fresh cigar from a humidor. "Smoke, Mr. Bernardi?" he asks pleasantly.

"No, thanks," I say. He lights up as I continue. "They also give him a great deal of money. It will help him make a new start in a new country away from the claws of the Los Angeles police. He's being set up like duck pins in a bowling alley but he's too dumb or too scared to see it. "

"Yes, not perceptive at all," Overton says, blowing smoke in my direction. In reality he's been doing this ever since we sat down but this is the first time he's had a lit cigar in his hand. "Now, let me guess what's next," Overton continues. "As soon as he's across the border, someone calls the Tijuana police and tells them there's a fugitive gringo in their midst wandering around with thousands and thousands of Yankee dollars."

"Right," I say with a grin. "You'd make a good screenwriter, Lieutenant. So anyway the anonymous cop gives the Mexican police a perfect description of Angel---"

"Just a minute," Overton says. "You didn't say it was the cop that made the call."

"My mistake. Sure it was the cop. The same caller that tipped the L.A. Times. Same soft spoken educated voice. And of course, it works. They find him right away, grab the money, toss him in a jail cell and then realize they'd be much better off if Angel escaped so they could eliminate him and keep the money free and clear. No muss. No fuss."

"Makes sense."

"Yes, so they leave the cell door open and Angel walks out but then he spoils everything by actually escaping Tijuana and making his way to Ensenada where he calls a trusted friend, we'll call him Ally, and arrangements are made to pick him up by boat and bring him back to Los Angeles because by now Angel is very aware his so-called friends have betrayed him."

"It took him long enough," Overton says, leaning back in his chair.

"Well, no one ever said he was real sharp and to prove it, he does something really dumb. He calls his boyfriend at the ranch in Texas because he is sure the boyfriend is worried about him, which he isn't. And he tells the boyfriend about the escape plan from Ensenada. So as soon as Angel hangs up, the boyfriend calls Abigail, the mastermind, who calls Avaricious, the cop, who calls the Tijuana cops and tells them where to go and what time to be there. Are you following all this, Lieutenant?" I ask.

"Like a beagle chasing the fox," he says. "Your friend has a vivid imagination."

"Agreed," I say. "Now here's where it gets tricky."

Overton leans forward in his chair, checking his watch. His expression has changed from feigned interest to obvious boredom. "No, Mr. Bernardi, this whole pipe dream of yours has been tricky since the moment we sat down. Is there much more of this nonsense, because I have a lunch date."

"Sure, Lieutenant, I'll cut to the last scenes. You're probably wondering how I know for sure that the cop is involved in this up to his eyeballs."

"Actually I'm not but continue. I'll give you five more minutes and then I'm going to have to leave. And by the way, you can cut the crap. Let's start using real names."

"Why not?" I say. "When the Tijuana cops bungle the hit job and Hubbell ends up back in the States in protective custody, you and Elvira have a major problem. Not to worry. You're getting paid a lot to deal with major problems so you arrange for a shyster lawyer to spring Hubbell loose and as the key police officer involved you can avoid some of the legalities. But once again Hubbell slips past you. Eventually you use his beloved boyfriend Boyd Larrabee, who has flown in from Texas, to draw him into the open and finally you have him in your clutches."

Overton gets up from his chair and walks over to the coat rack where he slips into his shoulder holster. He pops open the cylinder to make sure he has a full load. He smiles at me in the process.

I continue. "I make a pretty good guess that he's been taken to the beach house in Malibu and I call you because I haven't yet stumbled to the fact that you're one of the bad guys. You tell me you'll take care of it and for me to keep out of it which I am not going to do. You say you will call the Sheriff and have a county squad car on the scene right away."

Overton walks over to a nearby bookcase which holds a tray with a water pitcher and a couple of glasses. He takes a couple of white pills from his shirt pocket and washes them down. He smiles at me again. "Aspirin. You're giving me a headache."

"By the time I get to the beach house it's dark out. I find Boyd Larrabee dead in the den and Hubbell Cox dead in the bedroom with a suicide note by his side. I realize someone else is in the house and I try to hide but Willie Babbitt finds me and tries to chase me down with the intent of blowing my brains out."

"Whereupon I show up," Overton says, "and save your miserable ungrateful life. No thanks necessary. All in the line of duty. It's been fascinating." He moves to his office door. "I'm off to lunch. If you're not out of here in three minutes a couple of large police officers will show up to escort you to the parking lot."

"You got tripped up by the squad car. That's how I was able to nail you."

"So now I've been nailed. This gets better and better."

"It was still light when you said you were going to contact the Sheriff's office yet the call to respond to the beach house didn't come through until the deputies were cleaning up a gang fight at Zuma Beach long after it was dark. You had no intention of letting the Sheriff's Department screw up your plan. Hubbell with a suicide note was good. Willie Babbitt full of bullet holes was even better."

"I didn't have to shoot him," Overton says.

"Oh, yes, you did. My corpse dead in the sand would have

raised a lot more questions than you were prepared to deal with."

Overton smiles again but this one is cold. "Congratulations, Mr. Bernardi. You are a wonderful story teller.And now, at long last, are you through?" Overton asks from the open doorway.

"I am," I say, rising from my chair.

"And how do you expect to prove this fanciful tale?" he asks.

"I don't. I can't."

"Yes, I though not," Overton says.

I walk to the doorway and belly my way past him. "But it is a helluva story, Lieutenant, and I'm old school. I believe if you tell a good story often enough to more and more people, sooner or later someone is going to wonder if maybe there isn't a little truth mixed in with all that so-called fiction. And once people start wondering and questioning, well, Lieutenant, anything is possible." I smile. "You take care now." And with that I walk off. I wait for the bullet in my back. It never comes.

Back at the studio I stride through the anteroom to my office with only a perfunctory smile in Glenda Mae's direction. She's seen this look before so she keeps her mouth shut. I am mad and getting madder.

I sit down at my typewriter and roll in a sheet of plain white paper. This may not be the smartest thing I'm about to do but I'm tired of being treated like road kill. I'm furious at Elvira for engineering Bryce's death. Not even the worst of us deserves to be murdered. I'm furious at Willie, a man of no conscience, who had the blood of three men on his hands when he died. I'm furious with Lloyd Overton who is supposed to protect and serve and who took all of us, especially me, for simpletons. And most of all, I guess, I am furious with Bunny who has dumped me like last week's macaroni and cheese. And of them all, this is the one that hurts the most.

I start to type:

"Personal to Chief William Parker. Read only if you are absolutely serious about weeding out the bad apples in your department....."

I type up the scenario more or less as I told it to Overton in his office. I leave my name out because I'm fed up with everything about this case. From here on it's Parker's problem. He'll either look into it or he won't. His call. Maybe justice will be done. More likely not but that's something Parker will have to answer for, not me. I'm not a policeman or a District Attorney or a member of a jury or a sitting judge. It's their responsibility now and deep down I pray that this is one of those cases that prove that Justice is more than just a seven letter word. I type Chief Parker's name and address on a plain white envelope and I affix a first class stamp. I take it out to the ante room and hand it to Glenda Mae. She takes it from me as if it were radioactive.

"Drop it in a mailbox on the way home," I say. Then I add, "Please."

"My pleasure, boss," she says. "May I ask----?"

"No!" I growl.

"Gotcha," she says slipping the envelope into her purse.

There is a rap on the door jamb behind me and I turn to see this pleasant looking guy framed in the doorway. He has a toothy smile. I don't know why but I'm always suspicious of toothy smiles.

"Mr. Bernardi?" he asks stepping into the room.

"I'm Joe Bernardi," I say.

He puts out his hand. We shake.

"Tad Pasternak, The Times-Union, Albany, New York."

"Nice to meet you, Tad. Did we have an appointment?"

He shakes his head. "No, I just slipped onto the studio

grounds on my own. I've sort of been promoted and given a really important assignment by the home office."

I'm puzzled. "Home office?"

"The Hearst Corporation, sir. They own the Times-Union and, uh, I guess some of the big shots kind of like the way I write because they want to syndicate my column to the other Hearst papers."

I smile knowingly. "You mean they're tapping you to replace Bryce Tremayne."

He gives me a toothy aw-shucks grin. "Well, sir, nobody can really replace Mr. Tremayne. I mean, he was so special. But they do want me to get the interview."

"And what interview is that, Tad?" I ask in my silkiest voice.

"Why, Elia Kazan, of course. In a couple of months he'll be up in front of HUAC but before that, we want to get in our own licks at that Commie sympathizer."

I nod sagely and turn to Glenda Mae.

"Glenda Mae?"

"Yes, boss?" she smiles, fluttering her eyes in anticipation.

"Did you hear what that man said?"

"I did," she says.

"And what are you going to do about it?" I ask.

"Call security?" she asks hesitantly.

"Good girl," I say.

"Thank you, boss," she says, still smiling, as she reaches for the phone.

THE END

AUTHOR'S NOTE

"A Streetcar Named Desire" was, indeed, a very special motion picture and received a host of Oscar nominations including Best Picture. But a funny thing happened on the way to the ceremony. "An American in Paris" was named Best Picture, George Stevens was named Best Director for "A Place in the Sun" and Humphrey Bogart won his long overdue Best Actor Oscar for "The African Queen". On the plus side, the other awards for Acting went to Vivien Leigh, Karl Malden and Kim Hunter. Brando would be nominated the next three years in succession, finally winning in 1954 for "On The Waterfront", directed by his good friend, Elia Kazan, who was also honored as Best Director to the applause of many and the consternation of others. Kazan had finally been brought before HUAC in 1952 and as he had promised, he cooperated by naming names. He was vilified in some circles and it is thought that "On the Waterfront" (about a long-shoreman who turns informer against a crooked labor leader) was his way of justifying his actions before the committee. Vivien Leigh continued to suffer from bipolar disorder and her work became more and more sporadic. In 1967 she died due to complications with tubercolosis. As always, this novel is total fiction and scenes involving real persons are complete fabrications and are meant in no way to denigrate or demean.

MISSING SOMETHING?

The first three books in the Hollywood Murder Mystery series are still available from Grove Point Press at a low introductory price of $9.95 each. All copies will be personally signed and dated by the author. If you purchase ALL THREE at $29.85 for the set, you will automatically become a member of "the club". This means that you will be able to buy all subsequent volumes at the $9.95 price , a savings of $3.00 over the regular cover price of $12.95. This offer is confined to direct purchases from The Grove Point Press and does not apply to other on-line sites which may carry the series.

Book One—1947
JEZEBEL IN BLUE SATIN

WWII is over and Joe Bernardi has just returned home after three years as a war correspondent in Europe. Married in the heat of passion three weeks before he shipped out, he has come home to find his wife Lydia a complete stranger. It's not long before Lydia is off to Reno for a quickie divorce which Joe won't accept. Meanwhile he's been hired as a publicist by third rate movie studio, Continental Pictures. One night he enters a darkened sound stage only to discover the dead body of ambitious, would-be actress Maggie Baumann. When the police investigate, they immediately zero in on Joe as the perp. Short on evidence they attempt to frame him and almost succeed. Who really killed Maggie? Was it the over-the-hill actress trying for a comeback? Or the talentless director with delusions of grandeur? Or maybe it was the hapless leading man whose career is headed nowhere now that the "real stars" are coming back from the war. There is no shortage of suspects as the story speeds along to its exciting and unexpected conclusion.

Book Two—1948
WE DON'T NEED NO STINKING BADGES

Joe Bernardi is the new guy in Warner Brothers' Press Department so it's no surprise when Joe is given the unenviable task of flying to Tampico, Mexico, to bail Humphrey Bogart out of jail without the world learning about it. When he arrives he discovers that Bogie isn't the problem. So-called accidents are occurring daily on the set, slowing down the filming of "The Treasure of the Sierra Madre" and putting tempers on edge. Everyone knows who's behind the sabotage. It's the local Jefe who has a finger in every illegal pie. But suddenly the intrigue widens and the murder of one of the actors throws the company into turmoil. Day by day, Joe finds himself drawn into a dangerous web of deceit , dupliciity and blackmail that nearly costs him his life.

Book Three—1949
LOVE HAS NOTHING TO DO WITH IT

Joe Bernardi's ex-wife Lydia is in big, big trouble. On a Sunday evening around midnight she is seen running from the plush offices of her one- time lover, Tyler Banks. She disappears into the night leaving Banks behind, dead on the carpet with a bullet in his head. Convinced that she is innocent, Joe enlists the help of his pal, lawyer Ray Giordano, and bail bondsman Mick Clausen, to prove Lydia's innocence, even as his assignment to publicize Jimmy Cagney's comeback movie for Warner's threatens to take up all of his time. Who really pulled the trigger that night? Was it the millionaire whose influence reached into City Hall? Or the not so grieving widow finally freed from a loveless marriage. Maybe it was the partner who wanted the business all to himself as well as the new widow. And what about the mysterious envelope, the one that disappeared and everyone claims never existed? Is it the key to the killer's identity and what is the secret that has been kept hidden for the past forty years?

Order any one of the above for the low introductory price of $9.95. Order all three for $29.85 and "join the club" giving you the privilege of purchasing all subsequent books in the series for $9.95 as opposed to the cover price of $12.95. This offer applies only to purchases made directly by check or money order to The Grove Point Press, P.O.Box 873, Pacific Grove, CA 93950. All books personally signed by the author. The price per book includes all taxes as well as shipping and handling.

AVAILABLE NOW
Book Four—1950
EVERYBODY WANTS AN OSCAR

After six long years Joe Bernardi's novel is at last finished and has been shipped to a publisher. But even as he awaits news, fingers crossed for luck, things are heating up at the studio. Soon production will begin on Tennessee Williams' "The Glass Menagerie" and Jane Wyman has her sights set on a second consecutive Academy Award. Jack Warner has just signed Gertrude Lawrence for the pivotal role of Amanda and is positive that the Oscar will go to Gertie. And meanwhile Eleanor Parker, who has gotten rave reviews for a prison picture called "Caged" is sure that 1950 is her year to take home the trophy. Faced with three very talented ladies all vying for his best efforts, Joe is resigned to performing a monumental juggling act. Thank God he has nothing else to worry about or at least that was the case until his agent informed him that a screenplay is floating around Hollywood that is a dead ringer for his newly completed novel. Will the ladies be forced to take a back seat as Joe goes after the thief that has stolen his work, his good name and six years of his life?

COMING SOON!
Book Six—1952
NICE GUYS FINISH DEAD

ABOUT THE AUTHOR

Peter S. Fischer is a former television writer-producer who currently lives with his wife Lucille in the Monterey Bay area of Central California. He is a co-creator of "Murder,She Wrote" for which he wrote over 40 scripts. Among his other credits are a dozen "Columbo" episodes and a season helming "Ellery Queen". He has also written and produced several TV miniseries and Movies of the Week. In 1985 he was awarded an Edgar by the Mystery Writers of America. "The Unkindness of Strangers" is the fifth in a series of murder mysteries set in post WWII Hollywood and featuring publicist and would-be novelist, Joe Bernardi.

TO ORDER ADDITIONAL COPIES

If your local bookseller is out of stock, you may order additional copies of this book through The Grove Point Press, P.O. Box 873, Pacific Grove, California 93950. Enclose check or money order for $12.95. We pay shipping, handling and any taxes required. Order 3 or more copies and take a 10% discount. 8 or more, take 20%. You may also obtain copies via the internet through Amazon and other sites which offer a paperback edition as well as electronic versions. All copies purchased directly from The Grove Point Press will be personally signed and dated by the author.